A HIGHLANDER'S REDEMPTION

HIGHLANDS EVER AFTER

AILEEN ADAMS

A HIGHLANDER'S REDEMPTION

Book One of the *Highlands Ever After* Series!

Like battles, some redemptions cannot be won...

In early 1746, Alasdair Macintyre is headed home after the rout at Culloden on Drummossie Moor, in sight of Inverness. The battle has been lost and scar on his face that makes him so ferocious-looking that even children run from him in terror. He learns his father has betrothed him to a local lass—a nearly blind woman—in exchange for a sizeable dowry and a chunk of land. The woman brings with her a companion that hates him immediately.

He has no interest in having a chain around his neck, not

even in the form of a woman he once knew as a girl—a gangly, twig of a girl.

When Alasdair learns the English government has sent agents to look for those who fought on the side of Bonnie Prince Charlie his ire arises. An ire that is even more enflamed by a vision from the local sheriff who offers a thinly veiled warning that there is a price of his head.

But Beitris is no longer the girl Alasdair Macintyre remembers. She's blossomed into a stunning woman, though one that is terrified of the scarred Highlander she's betrothed to. When Beitris learns of the treachery behind the one who has given up Alasdair to the English she's forced to make a decision. One between her family and the gruff, scarred soldier she's begun to love.

1

Alasdair Macintyre knew soon after the battle began that the effort had been in vain. That they'd come out to this field to be slaughtered, that nothing would be gained and all might be lost.

Were the men around him as aware of this as he was? They were outnumbered, outmatched. Certainly, there was more than enough bravery and vigor, but there was little good that bravery and vigor could do in the face of well-trained, well-suited men intent on dispatching with their foe.

Unfortunately, the English were better prepared for this, slicing through the Scottish ranks as one might slice through a loaf of bread no matter how bravely his brethren fought.

He raised his sword, the sword of his father and grandfather, slashing downward upon the shoulder of an Englishman. The man screamed, blood spurting from the wound even before Alasdair pulled the sword's blade free with a great sucking sound audible even over the sound of so many roars and screams, the pounding of hooves.

He turned, raising his wooden shield to block the swinging of a mace aimed at his head. Upon blocking the blow, which reverberated through his arm and shoulder, he raised his head and slashed with his sword again and again. He slashed until his foe no longer stood, his arm aching from the effort.

It mattered not. The desire to live, to survive this, overrode every other urge and desire. He simply had to defend his life. He refused to die.

Though so many fell around him. So very many. Only minutes had passed since the start of the battle, and already it was impossible to move forward without stepping or even falling over the bodies. The severed limbs. One lad wept, crying out for his mother in a pitiful voice.

What was it all for? Why had they embarked upon this?

A roar came from behind him. He spun, eyes wide, barely able to raise his shield as an English broadsword came down in a decisive arc. The man wielding the weapon mattered not.

At first, he believed the blade had missed him. How such a thing would be possible, he did not know. He only knew the sword completed its arc, and that the wide-eyed man—barely more than a lad, Alasdair noted somewhere in his mind—appeared prepared to strike again.

All of this went past his awareness in the moment it took for the pain to make itself known. Yes, the blade had struck home, and had the man wielding the sword been much nearer, he might have taken Alasdair's head off.

Though he'd done damage enough. The wound extended from well up on Alasdair's head, in his hair, down the side of his face and along his jaw.

The pain was fire, as though flames licked his flesh. He covered the wound with one hand, seeking to staunch the flow of hot blood which already splashed across his tunic and cloak. He might as well have tried to hold back the tide, for blood flowed between his fingers, over the top of his hand. He tasted it, smelled it, the entirety of his existence was nothing but pain and blood.

His opponent had moved on, having considered him no longer a danger. Perhaps the Englishman was correct, for all that was left for Alasdair to do was stagger amongst the dead and dying, his feet sliding in the blood-soaked mud. All that mattered was getting away, stopping the blood before it was too late. He would bleed to death here, in this field, among so many others whose blank eyes had once held a spark of life.

Perhaps it was already too late, for his legs threatened to weaken until they could no longer support him. Indeed, his body sagged, his legs bowing. *Push on, push on*, he told himself, all but shouting to be heard over the screaming, shrieking, burning pain in his face.

Yet his body had other ideas, indeed, for it was not long before his legs gave out entirely. He had bled too much, the evidence of it now soaking through his cloak, his tunic, the warmth now spreading over his chest. His face had been all but flayed open, his hand now holding part of it in place.

He collapsed, falling onto his back, his head resting upon the thigh of a dead man. Scot or Englishman, it mattered not. The man was dead, as Alasdair would soon be.

None of this would have come to pass had he never joined this effort.

It was easy, truly, to imagine himself on the farm as he stared up at the sky. So blue, just as it had been in his youth. All the times he'd slipped away from chores, escaping on his own. Lying on his back beneath the withered, old tree which he'd claimed as his own, one which would never bear fruit nor even flower again. One which by all accounts ought to have been removed as it no longer served its intended purpose.

Yet it had not been, which to a lad had served as further proof that the tree was meant always to be his. He'd gone there so many times, to rest beneath its leafless branches. To hide at times, yes, to escape. To ponder. A lad needed a place where he might simply be alone, to nurse his hurts where none would see.

He might be there now, in fact. The sky appeared just the same. All the moment lacked was the sound of the winding stream which strayed quite near where the tree had grown and died.

Yes, if he listened harder to the sound of blood rushing in his ears than he did to the sounds of men in various stages of dying, he could imagine himself there. Where he so wished to be. Where life was peaceful, where he did not drip precious blood onto the ground beneath him. Where his very existence was not in question.

If only he'd remained there. If only he had never strayed from that precious place. He ought to have known better than to believe this madness would result in anything positive. The English would always win in the end, as they ever had.

The pain in his face had dulled from the most excruciating thing he'd ever known or had ever imagined to something manageable, something which faded to the background. He was dying. This was the end of his life. Indeed, he felt himself slipping away, felt the world growing dim.

If only he could have made it to the farm, and his stream and his tree. Just once more.

2

The sun was warm on Beitris's hands as she dug for new potatoes on a morning in late spring. The entire world smelled of life, new and fresh and full of promise. She smiled at the feeling of a worm crawling across the back of her fingers, its home having been overturned by her work.

"Forgive me," she murmured to the worm, which undoubtedly had burrowed its way back into the dirt.

"What did ye say?" asked Elspeth, her companion. Judging from the way her voice carried, she was a few rows away, likely digging among the onions.

"Nothing worth minding," Beitris smiled. Elspeth did not think much of her penchant for speaking to mindless creatures, for engaging with birds and squirrels and even mice. She believed her charge to be a bit addled in this respect, wondering aloud at times whether it was only her eyesight which had failed her over her lifetime.

Elspeth could not understand. She was a woman of great logic and strong opinion. Once she'd decided upon a point, there was little to no chance of changing her mind. She possessed a great deal of patience, certainly—were it not for that patience, Beitris would be lost in a world her eyes could not perceive.

Yet she had little care for Beitris's understanding of that world. She understood not the impulse to speak to the birds which never failed to sing near the window in the morning. The presence of scraps of bread undoubtedly lured the birds, of course, but Beitris never failed to thank them for their song.

Elspeth could not understand, because she saw with her eyes and nothing else. She did not rely on her ears as Beitris did, nor on her other senses. She did not understand what it meant to rely on others so thoroughly. On their patience and kindness, on their generosity and gentleness.

The world could be cruel, indeed, to one without their sight. Beitris Boyd was well aware of how fortunate she was, and believed she ought to express her gratitude. Even to the mindless worm whose dark comfort she'd interrupted.

"How many have ye dug?" Elspeth called out.

Beitris ran her hands over the potatoes, spread out over an old length of linen. "Ten."

"A handful more ought to do it. Yer father and his riders shall be possessed of a terrible hunger upon their return." Indeed, they had been away from the family home for nearly a fortnight. Just why it had been of such importance to ride out with little announcement, neither of them could say. They were not often made privy to the reasons behind such decisions.

"Perhaps they shall bring reports from the battles in the south," Beitris suggested, her fingers fumbling in the sun-warmed soil until she unearthed another potato.

"Aye, little good it shall do," Elspeth muttered. "For once we've heard of it, something else has taken place. Why, the Jacobite revolt might be entirely over at this moment, and we would not know of it."

Would that it were the case, though Beitris doubted any such thing would come to pass. The way the men spoke as they sat around her father's table, the passion with which they argued bitterly against English rule. The war would never end if these men had any say in it, unless England were entirely defeated.

Which, in her heart of hearts, Beitris doubted. For she'd heard her father's private thoughts, as well, shared only with his most trusted steward. It was not as if she plotted to overhear private conversations. She simply could not help it, for her hearing had strengthened in response to the loss of her sight.

Sight which had never been as strong as it might, even from birth. Sight which had almost entirely left her by the time she'd passed the fourth winter after her birth. Now, nearly seventeen years after that, she was only aware of bright light—if she turned her face toward the sun, her field of vision lightened—and of some color. The green of new leaves, the red of blood. The darkness of her own hair, though even that was only possible when she stood in the presence of the sun.

Her hearing was unmatched, however. She heard the soft mumblings which Elspeth emitted under her breath as she worked, making lists of the many tasks left to accomplish before the men of the house returned. She heard the nighttime sounds of the household, the breathing and snoring and other, unsavory sounds which she only wished she could ignore. She could hear the approach of a horse long before the beast made itself visible to anyone around her.

And she'd heard Bruce Boyd, her father, express his secret doubts. Where would Scotland be if the war were lost? What would become of them?

What would become of her?

Yet another fact of her life which Beitris knew might easily have not been true were it not for patience and generosity. Many was the man who might have sent her away, who might have regarded her as nothing but a burden. She was sightless, and a lass on top of that. There was no reason for him to see to her education or her care.

Elspeth had reminded her of this more than once, especially when her father's decisions regarding her future had caused her grief. "He might not care, Beitris," she would croon, stroking Beitris's hair. "He might have abandoned ye, but he didna. He merely wishes to ensure ye are not left alone once he is gone to his reward."

Yes, and who would agree to a marriage with a blind lass? It could not have been a simple matter for him to arrange. She was grateful he had not brought it into conversation as of late, for talk of it only ever fell into argument.

She did not believe she needed to be wed, and would certainly not wed the first likely lad who came along simply because he did not refuse her. And not because her father wished to remove her from his conscience, either.

Though it did cause her pain, true pain, when she considered the burden she must be on him. He feared for her future, for what might become of her once he'd gone on to his reward. She was not a son. She could not inherit the land, anything of his.

If only the law would change. Her troubles would be over.

"What do ye find so amusing, I'd like to know?" Elspeth grumbled as she worked her way to her feet. Years spent scrubbing stone floors before becoming Beitris's companion and guardian had left her with knees which seemed ever to ache.

"Did I laugh? I was not aware." Beitris gathered together the corners of the linen sheet, bringing the potatoes together in the center that she might carry them into the kitchen.

"Ye had best contain such moments of mirth if ye know what is best for ye," Elspeth advised. She held her elbow out to the side, that Beitris might take hold and be led to the kitchen.

"Ye fear my da will believe I've gone daft in his absence?" she teased, delighting in the way her friend snorted in derision. "Perhaps I shall. Perchance if he finds me daft, he shall no longer wish to secure a husband."

"Och, say no such thing," Elspeth hissed. "There are worse things for a lass than to be wed, ye ought to know. There are times when I, too, ask myself whether ye have gone daft. Why do ye insist upon raising such trouble for yer da?"

"Dinna pretend as though ye believe I ought to be wed to simply any man." Once they were safely inside, Beitris could manage on her own. She knew the kitchen by heart, could make her way without jostling or toppling anything.

If anyone who did not know her to be blind observed her, she would wager they would believe her to be seeing.

She placed the potatoes near a bucket of water, rolling up her sleeves and tucking them in place. "Ye have felt the same as I lo these many moons," she reminded Elspeth while setting upon the task of washing and quartering.

"Aye, I have at that," Elspeth agreed, standing several paces from where Beitris worked. "Yet ye canna wait for always, my dear. Ye must have a husband, though ye might not wish for one as yet."

"Why must I? Truly, can ye give reason why I must?"

"Dinna ye wish to have a home of yer own, lassie?" Rarely did Elspeth take this tone with her, so soft and serious. There was no secret of how the older woman felt toward her—as a mother, or nearly. It ought not to have come as a surprise that she would speak so.

Yet it tightened Beitris's heart, just the same, and brought a stinging sort of feeling to her eyes.

"What of it?" Beitris whispered, scrubbing as she had never scrubbed a potato in her life.

"Dinna ye wish to one day have a bairn? Perhaps many bairns?"

Her hand slipped, sending the potato splashing into the water, sprinkling her face. When Elspeth touched her, like as not intending to wipe her dry, she flinched back. "Nay, I might do it for myself."

"Dinna ye take such a tone of voice with me, lassie."

She drew a deep breath, letting it out slowly as she used her apron to wipe her face. "Aye, I wish to have a bairn for my own, someday," she admitted as she wiped. "Ye ken well my feelings."

"How do ye intend to—"

"I dinna know," Beitris all but growled. "Tis not reason enough for me to wed any man willing to be my husband. What if he is cruel? What if he wishes to take advantage of me?"

"I pity the man who believes he might take advantage of ye," Elspeth assured her. "And ye shall go nowhere without myself beside ye. I would wear the hide from any man who dared harm ye, my dear."

Beitris believed this with all her heart, which was why she smiled.

"The master has returned!" The message echoed through the halls of the household, passed from one maid to another after the first had announced it from a high window. "The master and his men have returned!"

"We must be swift," Elspeth sighed. Beitris heard her

knife slicing through onions, potatoes. "I might have known they would arrive earlier than intended. Yer da is a fine man, but he is determined to make my life difficult."

Beitris could relate.

They finished preparing the vegetables in time for one of the kitchen lasses to add them to the big, steaming pot hung over the fire. Boar stewed there, cooking slowly over many hours. The men would be of great hunger, no doubt. She hoped to have some for herself, though she knew she'd be fortunate to spear a few leftover bits.

"Where is my Beitris?" Bruce Boyd's voice carried to every corner of the house as he stormed in. This was his natural state of being, or so it seemed. Ever shouting, even when he was not in a foul temper. As if he hoped to make up for slightness of stature with the loudness of his voice.

"Ye had best not keep him waiting," Elspeth advised.

Beitris dried her hands on her apron and smoothed down any stray bits of hair which had escaped her braid while working in the garden. She needed no guidance while inside the house, unless the floors were fresh-scrubbed and still wet. Otherwise, it was no matter for her to move about freely.

She found him in his study. "Da? Ye have returned. A blessing, to be certain." He smelled of horses and sweat and sunshine and wine. A familiar combination.

"Aye, Beitris. Tis yourself I wish most to speak with. Come, be seated." She heard several men shifting in place to allow her through. "The rest of ye, leave us."

It was with knocking knees that she sat in a small,

wooden chair near the fire. Her hands trembled; she folded them in her lap, pressing the palms together as tightly as she could to keep them still.

"Lass, we have spoken many times of this, and ye have driven me to anger many times," her father began in a gruff voice. "Yet ye shall see in time that I have done ye a good deed."

"What have ye done, then?" she asked in a voice that shook nearly as badly as her hands. She tried to sound as though she found this amusing, though the truth was anything but.

"I have found a husband for ye." He lifted one of her hands and pressed a cup into it. "Drink, lass. Tis a grand day for ye."

As if she could. How would one swallow with such a lump in their throat? "Who?" she managed to whisper, her heart sinking. Elspeth ought to have joined her. She longed for someone to understand, to sit by her side.

Now, she was alone. Utterly and truly.

"Ye shall make a fine bride," Bruce Boyd decided. She heard him gulp down his ale before pouring another cup. "Aye, ye have made me proud already. Tis a fine arrangement."

"Who?" she asked again, her voice stronger this time. It was torture, plain and simple, and he insisted on making it worse.

"Alasdair Macintyre."

She reeled. "He... was rumored killed, was he not?"

"Aye, so we were told. His da received word not a fortnight past from his son, speaking of injury but vowing his return. Word came to the house while the men and myself were beneath the roof that Alastair had been seen and spoken to in Edinburgh, and that he was riding north."

"And ye wish me to marry him?"

"I wish it, as does old Angus. The man is not long for this world, they say, and t'would do his heart good to know his son would be settled with a wife before he goes on to his reward."

Was this supposed to make her feel better? To boost her spirits? Nothing could have been further from the case. Her insides were frozen in spite of the fire.

Her husband. He'd been wounded badly enough that rumor of his death had spread to the highlands. Now, they were to be wed.

"What ails ye, lass?" her father boomed. "Tis a day of celebration! Ye ought to be thankin' me for going out of my way to secure your happiness."

"Happiness," she whispered, daring a sip of the ale still waiting in the cup. Why not? If there was ever a time to indulge herself, it was now.

3

I
t was a cool morning in late spring when Alasdair rode the last few miles to the farm he'd dreamt of every night since nearly dying on the field of battle. There'd been moments when he'd been near to giving up hope of ever seeing the place again, when the rain had fallen hard enough to leave travel an impossibility. There had been little hope of riding through such thick, impass-able mud.

Yet he'd managed it. He'd arrived at last. A tear came to his eye when he spied the house ahead, half-hidden in morning mist.

To have what his heart had yearned for most painfully was almost too much to bear.

He was hardly half the man he'd been upon leaving nearly a year ago. A man who had not inspired the tears of children, the gasps and cries of horror from lasses. Even men averted their gaze, cursing under their breath. In disgust, in pity.

To think, there'd been a time when he'd looked upon his arrival as a means of returning to the home he'd loved so deeply, where he'd known his life's only happiness. He'd looked back upon the farm and the great house as a heaven where he might find peace and contentment.

Now? Now, it was a refuge. The notion of locking himself behind the heavy door and closing the shutters against the world's inquiring gaze struck him as quite sensible, indeed. Perhaps necessary. He'd been reminded more times than he cared to recall just how hideous a face he'd been left with after that dreadful, useless battle.

He might smash the looking glass in his bedchamber, at that. For why should he wish to gaze upon himself? He was a twisted, unnatural creature who would never been gazed upon with anything less than horror.

Never had a sight stirred such emotion in his breast, then, as the sight of his home as it revealed itself to him. His salvation existed behind those walls. Walls which had stood for centuries, solid and sturdy. Walls which had held happy families, hardworking people. The home from which his father had managed the farm and surrounding lands since he'd come of age.

It would be Alasdair's to manage, one day. And the family line would end there. He would certainly never sire an heir. Not now.

He could not help but ask himself why all was so quiet that morning. Normally, there would be a great deal of activity. Stable lads shouting to one another, chickens running through the courtyard. The heavy clang of the blacksmith as he worked, the chatter and laughter of the household lasses.

There was hardly a sound coming from behind the walls surrounding the keep and its outer structures. It was nearly enough to cause him great concern as he dismounted with no one to look after his mount. There was not a stable lad in sight. No one at all to greet him.

He provided water for the overworked beast before striding into the keep. The fires had not been tended in far too long—in fact, very little had been tended. He heard much whispering and murmuring coming from the great hall and followed the sound, prepared to tear heads from shoulders.

Until he realized the whispering and murmuring was the result of prayer.

Prayer? He dared steal a glance through the half-open door and found no less than the entire household employed in beseeching the Good Lord to spare the life of...

The life of...

He backed away from the door and ran for the stone stairs, taking them two at a time before tearing down the corridor. His father's bedchamber sat at the far end, the doors standing open and faint light shining within.

Alasdair took pains to keep his face hidden upon entering, knowing how any of the women within might startle at the sight of him. There were three of them in all, their faces familiar, and they tended what appeared to be little more than a pile of bones beneath a layer of furs.

"Da?" he murmured, disbelieving. This? This was what his father had become in such a short time? This withered, frail creature?

The women looked toward him as one, all of them surprised at his sudden presence. Had they not gotten word of his approach? Perhaps not, if they were involved intently in the care of his father.

The father who attempted to lift his head from the pillow, but failed. "Alasdair? Ye have returned? Och, how I have prayed for this moment," he whispered with a faint smile. "How I prayed that I might set eyes upon ye once more."

Never had he known such a confusing, crushing mixture of emotion as he did upon approaching the bedside. "Da, I knew not..."

"Tis simple enough to ken," he whispered, patting the bed to invite his son to sit. "Ye have returned. I might rest easily, now, beside yer mam. She awaits me."

Alasdair's throat tightened. He knew not what to say, what even to think. Nothing could have prepared him for this. "Ye have ever been strong," he reminded the man. "Ye might be strong, still. Dinna cease hoping."

"Nay, nay. Tis prepared I am to go, and tired as well. I dinna wish to live longer. Tis the time for me to go." His eyes, once so bright and alive, were now flat and dull.

Yet they were as keen as ever. "Well? On with it, then. Show me that which ye have taken pains to conceal."

Alasdair's blood turned to ice. He cast a sidelong glance toward the women waiting at the other side of the bed. "Leave us for a time," he grunted, waving a hand. He did not wish for them to see him as yet. They appeared all too eager to leave the men on their own.

"We had word of a man riding north," his father explained in that same weak whisper. "One who'd suffered a terrible wound during battle. Whose face was dreadfully scarred. I take it t'was yourself of whom I heard."

Rather than explaining himself, Alasdair lowered his hood without another word. He bore the surprise which still managed to etch itself in the dying man's face. Surprise and dismay. "Och, lad," he croaked. "Tis worse than they described it."

"As ever, ye ken just what to say." Alasdair snickered. "Aye, 'tis dreadful."

"It matters not. Ye shall take yer place upon my death and ye shall provide heirs to secure our fortunes for generations. Just as ye are meant to do."

Alasdair stared at the man. Had he taken leave of his senses during his illness? That was the only explanation. "Da, I canna now. No lass... that is, I..."

"Did ye lose use of yer manhood, then?"

"Nay. Only my face was injured, though 'tis enough. Or have yer eyes failed ye?"

"Ye shall provide heirs, then. I might rest easy."

"What have ye done?" Alasdair whispered, his dismay growing with each moment that passed.

"I have arranged a wife for ye." A fit of coughing overcame him, leaving Alasdair waiting with bated breath to learn more.

Though he'd already heard more than enough to make his blood fairly boil in his veins. A wife? A wife! For him? Anyone who'd turned their gaze upon him along the long ride home had recoiled in horror. Word of his injury had spread faster than he could travel, so quickly that by the time he'd passed through the village on his way to the farm, he'd already heard word of his impending arrival.

By then, he'd traded with a merchant for a suitable cloak, one with a hood deep enough to hide most of his face. The fewer gasps of horror and disgust he was forced to hear, the better for everyone.

Once the racking, wet coughs had calmed, he leaned nearer his father. The man had shriveled, so much so that he scarcely looked to be half the size Alasdair remembered him. Such a change in half a year. "Ye arranged a wife? For me?" he asked.

"Aye," the dying man rasped. "Ye shall be wed. Ye shall provide an heir... as ye are meant to do."

"Nay, I shall not."

"Ye shall," his father insisted. "Tis yer duty, lad. It has ever been yer duty, since birth. Ye have always known it. Ye must provide an heir. Ye must be wed."

His fists clenched, twisting the sheet thrown over his father's shrunken body. "Who would wish to marry a man such as myself?" he growled, his heart racing sickeningly fast. "Who? Why would ye inflict this upon any lass?"

Was it illness that made the man behave so? Because

his thin lips twitched as though he tried to smile. He could not have been in his right mind. "One lass who shall not see ye, lad. She is the ideal bride for ye. Her father was here to visit me when we received word of yer return."

Alasdair's mind spun from this. Who could it be? Who could not see him? It made little sense.

Until... "Beitris Boyd? Was Bruce Boyd the man who visited here?" he asked, wishing it were not so but knowing it had to be.

"Aye." He smiled then, wider than Alasdair could recall his father ever smiling before. "Tis ideal. The lass is blind. Yer injury need not matter. She will ne'er see ye."

"She has lived in her father's house her entire life," Alasdair argued. He wished to scream, to shout, to tear the house down with his bare hands. Only his father's grave condition kept his temper in check. "She has been terribly closed away from the world. From people. None see her. I have not set eyes upon her in ten winters, at least."

More coughing. Alasdair could do nothing but sit and wait while the fit passed.

And fret. For her, for himself.

It was not fair. The lass was probably afraid of everything—she was blind, she knew only her father's house and land. She knew nothing of the surrounding area, the village.

She knew nothing of men. She could not possibly. Not in the manner which a man wished his bride to be innocent, either. She had likely never spoken to a man who was not her father or one of his trusted advisors. Perhaps a stable lad or a guard.

And she was to be his? He was not gentle. He was not kind. He was not meant to be married, especially not to a shy, frightened, blind lass who would like as not jump at the slightest noise.

It was cruel.

And there was nothing he could do about it. This arrangement would not have been announced to him had it not already been firmly set. Bruce Boyd was a clever man from what Alasdair recalled. He would not leave this to chance, especially when the daughter involved had lost her sight years earlier.

He would wish to be rid of her.

And Alasdair was the man who would take her as his bride.

Why had he struggled to survive if this was all life held for him?

4

———

"I dinna care for this."

Beitris's head snapped back harder and harder with each pass of the brush which Elspeth used on her long hair. "Might ye brush a bit more gently?" she had no choice but to ask, her teeth gritted against the pain in her scalp. "I feel the hair being ripped away."

"Och, forgive me." Still, Elspeth muttered this, angry. "How dare he? He has all but sold ye to the man without a care as to whether ye wish to wed him or nay."

"There is no need to remind me of this. I am well aware. There is little else I've thought about this past fortnight."

Had it truly only been a fortnight since word of Alasdair's return had reached them? In the weeks since, Bruce Boyd had all but burst with excitement and pride. To think, his daughter had managed to be promised in marriage to none other than a Macintyre.

Considering the fact that he'd never expected to

arrange such a fortunate match or any match at all, this was quite the victory for him.

Beitris, meanwhile, could think of nothing but what they'd heard about her future husband. She'd known him only slightly in her girlhood, but from what she'd learned through Elspeth, he'd become little more than a monster who held the rest of his household in a grip of terror.

"Wee bairns run from him," Elspeth muttered. "He frightens them so. Not merely because of his fearful countenance, mind ye. He possesses a terrible temper. The lasses tremble when he passes them in the corridor."

"Ye need not speak of it any longer," Beitris whispered. "I implore ye."

Elspeth let out a deep sigh. "Och, my dear. Forgive me. Ye dinna need to hear this from me. I ken too well how frightened ye are."

"I am not frightened."

"Beitris—"

"I am not frightened!" She slammed her hands upon the dressing table for good measure. She could not see the thing, but she certainly felt the sting in her palms. "I am angry. I am dismayed. I am filled with dread. But I am not a bit frightened of the man."

"I believe ye," Elspeth whispered. "I shall not speak of it again."

Beitris fell silent, and before long, Elspeth returned to the task of preparing her for the first contact with her husband.

Her husband. The words seemed foreign, as if spoken in another language. A husband for her. Hers. Her own.

He would never be her own, and she knew it well. Nor did she wish for him to be. As far as it concerned Beitris, they might very well live in different parts of his keep and never speak to one another. It would matter nothing to her. If anything, she might prefer it.

Except when the time came to provide him with an heir.

Her palms went slick with sweat at the very notion of such a thing. She might not have been a worldly lass, but she knew well what it took to carry and bear a bairn. To imagine behaving as such with Alasdair...

She would not be forced to look upon him, at least. Little consolation, but she was not accustomed to consolation in her life. This was nothing new.

"At the very least, he is terribly uncouth and rough," Elspeth fretted. Beitris was hardly able to contain her frustration—only reminding herself of how the older woman cared for her, how good and kind she had always been, and of the fact that this mumbling and muttering was a reflection of that caring and kindness held her temper in place.

Alasdair Macintyre was not the only one in possession of a fearful temper.

"He has been to war," she reminded Elspeth while the hair brushing continued. "I canna imagine war would not change a man. Roughen him. If he is to be my husband, I need remind myself of this. I must be kind and understanding. If I am not, I shall only destroy any chance of living peacefully."

Elspeth fell silent for what felt like a long time, for as long as it took Beitris's terribly thick hair to be brought under control, smoothed and braided, then coiled at the nape of her neck. It was frightfully heavy, though she wished she might see it. It might have been quite bonny.

"Dinna ye wish for more than peace, lass?" Elspeth asked once finished. "Dinna ye wish for much more?"

The strangest thing happened then. Her chest tightened in a way it normally did when she made the mistake of pondering what she'd missed in life. "Wishing is a mistake," she whispered, which was what she normally told herself whenever she made such a mistake. "I canna wish. It causes pain."

"Lass. My dear." Elspeth's arms closed around her from behind in a gentle embrace. "I shall wish for ye, then."

"Do that." Beitris closed her eyes for only a moment, allowing herself to sink into her sadness for just that long. Any longer, and she may not be able to pull herself out of it.

"If only he shall treat ye kindly," Elspeth whimpered, trembling like a bairn. As if it were she, herself, preparing to be bound in marriage. As if she were the one about to find herself locked in an unbreakable arrangement.

"I pray he shall," Beitris admitted. "Every evening before sleep, I pray he shall be kind. That he shall be understanding. If he truly is as cruel and unfeeling as we have heard, I fear it shall not be a simple matter. Yet he might take it into his heart to treat me well. After all, this was arranged prior to his return. He had no say in this, as I have had no say. We might use that as a way to strike a kinship."

"Ye are truly a wonder," Elspeth marveled as she prepared Beitris's gown, the fabric's rustling giving her away. "I dinna know that I would be half as understanding as ye have been."

"There is nothing to be done." How many times had she reminded herself of this? Perhaps she might one day believe and accept this. Perhaps she might cease hoping and wishing, which it seemed she could not as yet.

"What is takin' ye?" Her father's booming voice rang out in the corridor, on the other side of the door to the bedchamber. "We are due to meet yer husband, lassie. Be quick about it, then!"

"The devil with him," Elspeth spat under her breath. "If 'tis of such importance, he might go alone. But then he could not sell ye—"

"Dinna speak this way," Beitris warned in a sharp voice. "Ye must not. I find this difficult enough."

Elspeth held her tongue while assisting Beitris in dressing. It took little time, just as it had taken little time to gather her things and pack them into a trunk. One single trunk carrying everything she owned. She might at least have her belongings around her, something to remind her of home.

Though home had hardly been a heaven.

The ride took little time—if anything, Beitris wished it might stretch longer, even with the discomfort of the bouncing wagon beneath her. It seemed someone had placed every rock and stone in the highlands along the road, just for her. A gift on the eve of her wedding.

"Ye had best behave yourself, lass," her father muttered from where he sat beside her, driving the team. "Dinna give me cause to regret this."

"I shall not," she murmured, hands clasped in her lap. It seemed a bonny day, the sky blue enough for her to have a sense of its brilliance. Sunlight warmed her skin, driving away the chill which had settled into her very bones.

Would she ever be in her father's presence again once the wedding took place? Was it terribly wicked of her to hope she would not be? No, he had not been as cruel as he might have, but there was little love between them. Nearly none. Once she was another man's bride and thus bound to him, she need never bother herself with Bruce Boyd again.

Was it wicked for her to smile? Perhaps. Yet it could not be helped. It seemed there was a ray of sunshine in the middle of so much disappointment, as the sun broke through clouds after a storm and lit everything around it.

"We are coming to the farm now," Bruce announced. "Och, 'tis a grand keep ye shall be mistress of, lass." Was there an edge of humor in his voice? Did he find this amusing? He reeked of ale, even this early in the day, so Beitris could only assume he'd been celebrating while she dressed and prepared for the journey.

"Tis quite large," Elspeth murmured behind her, seated in the wagon's box. "The walls surrounding the keep are thick, grey stone. Tis no need for such a grand house now, though. The family is not a bit as large as t'was once."

Yes, Beitris was aware of this. The Macintyres had once been known as well for their impressive landholdings as they were for the size of their family. It had not been unusual for a time to have ten or even twelve living children result from a single marriage.

This had changed from one generation to the next, however, until Leslie Macintyre had died in childbirth after bearing a single son. People spoke in whispers of how broken this had left her husband, Angus, a broken man. He'd imagined the lands passing to one of his brother's sons, but all were dead now. Disease and battle had thinned the line until only Alasdair survived—his father had passed on only three days after Alasdair's return.

So much space for a single man.

No. A man and his wife.

There was heather in the meadow, its scent carrying on the breeze and delighting her. She imagined long afternoons gathering it by the armful, its deep purple blanketing the ground. That might be visible to her weak eyes, especially in the sun. Roses grew elsewhere, and someone had recently turned one of the fields. Fresh, rich earth was a aroma she'd long been accustomed to.

Perhaps life might not be as difficult as her companion imagined it would. There might be means of enjoying herself, of taking pleasure in her days, just as she'd managed while living in her father's household.

There was much whispering as the wagon rolled up to

the stone walls Elspeth had described. She held her head high, refusing to bow under the weight of dread which now settled on her like a boulder. No, she would not allow them to know her true feelings. Instead, she smiled as if pleased and even excited over this turn of events.

"He shall meet ye inside," a lad mumbled from beside her, presumably taking the reins from her father.

Elspeth scoffed. "He does not see fit to greet his bride in the out of doors?" she muttered under her breath, for only Beitris to hear. She might have reminded her companion that Alasdair would like as not wish to remain concealed whenever possible, yet it seemed better to hold her tongue. No need to discuss such matters before the household servants.

She was the lady of the house, or would be soon enough. She must begin to think and behave as one.

"No need to assist me," she murmured to the lad standing there, sensing he wished to help her alight from the wagon. "I am able to move about on my own. Thank ye kindly."

The lad murmured something that sounded like acceptance before scurrying off to tend to the team.

Still, she required Elspeth's arm for guidance into the keep. There would come a time when familiarity would leave her moving about with ease, without assistance, but that time was far off. Bruce led the way, and Beitris could imagine his chest puffed out with pride, his smile stretching from ear to ear.

There was a sudden change in the air, and not only

because they'd stepped inside. She felt him before she heard his heavy footfalls, felt the strength and power of his presence. It was nearly enough to make her bowels turn to water, and only the clutching of Elspeth's hand over hers kept Beitris from picking up her skirts and running blindly out into the midday.

Alasdair Macintyre, her soon-to-be husband.

The time had come for them to meet as adults.

5

W ell. At least she was pleasant to look at.

Alasdair lifted his cup, gazing at his intended over the rim as he drank deeply. It would take a great deal of wine to soothe the ever-present ache in his breast. There had hardly been time to grieve—and even then, his grief was so thoroughly mixed with resentment and a sense of betrayal that it was impossible to feel as he assumed other men felt upon the loss of their father.

"Ye set a fine table," Bruce Boyd observed in his ever-loud voice. It set Alasdair's teeth on edge. How anyone could live under the same roof with such a man was a mystery he could not begin to fathom.

"Thank ye kindly," he grunted, as something must be said and the man evidently expected a reply. "Tis... only proper for my bride and her good father." The words stuck in his throat, his tongue thick and awkward. What a torment this was.

He took his meals in his chambers as of late. In fact, much of his time was spent there. Alone, behind a closed door. Away from the world. Where he might be away from the world, away from prying eyes and whispers and horrified stares.

He knew the lasses about the house dreaded his presence. He knew how he frightened them—when only a year earlier, they'd all but swooned when he'd passed, clamoring for his attention at meals. How fickle women were.

At least the woman seated to his right would never behave that way. She could not see the scar running down that side of his face, would never flinch or recoil when he made the mistake of stepping into the light. He need not duck his head or turn his face away while in her presence. A small consolation, along with her pleasing countenance.

A pity, really, that her blue eyes were all but sightless. They were clear, sparkling in the light from so many fat, dripping candles. "Careful," he grunted when she reached across the table, in the direction of one of them.

She turned her head slightly in his direction. "I beg your pardon?" Her voice was low and sweet, though it trembled slightly. So he frightened her as well as the others.

He shifted in his chair, now uncomfortable at having spoken up. They'd hardly exchanged more than a few words since her arrival, in spite of the fact that she sat close enough that their arms nearly brushed each other. "Ah, that is, ye were nearing the candle. I did not wish for ye to burn your hand."

Her rosy lips parted to allow a soft gasp. "Och, I thank ye. I can see the light, somewhat, and can avoid it. I wished to pour ale for myself. Would ye care for more?"

How could she possibly manage it? Hesitation stole his voice while Beitris reached out for the handle to the pitcher. She grasped it with confidence and lifted it while holding her cup in the other hand. Yes, that companion of hers had spent a great deal of time murmuring in the lass's ear after they'd sat down. She must have been explaining where items were located, that her mistress might find them.

He'd imagined they were whispering about him. How foolish. Though who would blame him when so much whispering had already been done, both behind his back and in front of him?

He did not notice he held his breath until she began to pour in a controlled manner, her lips moving as she counted to three in barely a whisper. Not a drop splashed out of the cup. "Might I pour for ye?" she offered again, her head turned toward him.

"Aye." He touched his cup to her hand to indicate its presence and watched, silent, as she poured again. She then returned the pitcher to its place, holding the cup out for him to take it. "I thank ye."

"Think nothing of it," she murmured. Were her cheeks flushed? It was the wine, he reasoned. "More roast?"

"Nay, I have had my fill." The lass lifted a slice of the

sizzling goat, fresh from the kitchen, and lowered it to her plate. He did not intend to stare, but there was no helping it. One would never know she was without sight.

"Ye shall find the lass quite able to fend for herself." Bruce laughed. So he'd been watching. And he found it amusing. "Ye need pay her no mind, I assure ye."

Beitris stiffened, though she spoke not a word. Her eyes were downcast, hands folded upon her lap. Elspeth, her companion—a large, stern-looking woman—cast a doleful eye upon Bruce.

Alasdair cleared his throat. "Why would I wish to pay no mind to my wife?" he asked, turning to him. It was rare that he relished the effect of his destroyed countenance. While he had never wished to frighten lasses and bairns to the point where they ran and wept, he rather enjoyed putting this coarse, thoughtless man in his place.

Bruce stammered, his face going a darker red than before. He reeked of wine and ale and was barely able to sit up straight. Alasdair had never cared much for men who were unable to hold their drink. "Ah. That is. Eh."

A soft voice rang out at his other side. "Think nothing of it," Beitris murmured. "He merely means to explain how independent I have become. Indeed, I am certain that with time I shall be able to make my way about the house on my own."

"Truly, then?" he asked. She had a way about her, this Beitris. A softness. She understood without being told how her father tried his patience. Perhaps he tried hers, as well.

He resented this man, doubly so as Angus had passed

on to whatever reward he'd earned. Bruce Boyd represented both men at once and both men had taken advantage. A blind daughter, a horribly disfigured son. A perfect match.

It was enough to make him want to overturn the table, to set fire to everything and laugh while it burned. This was what his life as the sole Macintyre heir had earned him. Forced into marriage with a lass who would never see him, because he was too horrifying to be seen.

Yet the lass was just as much a victim of this as he— more, in fact, since he understood now how little her father thought of her. To think of bragging about not paying her any mind.

She smiled, her gaze fixed on the candle's flame. "Aye. Ye need not trouble yourself. I shall be well. Elspeth looks after me." The older woman met his gaze over the top of Beitris's head, and there was not so much as a hint of warmth in her flinty eyes. She would be a formidable one, to be certain.

Once the meal was finished, which could not have come quickly enough as far as Alasdair was concerned, they retired to his study. His. No longer his father's. There had not yet been time to accustom himself to his new duties.

Beitris relied on Elspeth to lead her about, to guide her to a chair near the fire. He was unaware that he'd earned a guardian, as well. One who seemed to delight in eyeing him with suspicion. He'd never be free of her, either. Another curse on him.

He took the chair nearest his bride for the sake of propriety, knowing her father would never allow him to sit elsewhere. Now that they faced one another, he was better able to take in the full measure of the woman who would call this house her own.

A far cry from the awkward, freckled lass she was in her youth. She'd grown into a bonny thing, indeed, her hair gleaming in the firelight, full lips arranged in a soft smile. He asked himself if she meant that smile or if the smile was a means of concealing her true feelings.

It mattered little, he supposed. She would make a fair bride, smiling and quiet and minding herself. Elspeth might have been rather a fearsome thing, but she would make his life easier by guiding Beitris about until she became comfortable and confident.

Yes. This might be easier than he'd considered.

"Might I see ye?"

He blinked. "Eh?" Perhaps he'd misheard.

He had not. Beitris lifted her hands, reaching for him. "By touch. That I might see ye without use of my eyes."

"Tis how she sees others," Bruce muttered between gulps of wine. "Ye must accustom yourself to it."

It was clear the lass was not about to be ignored, no matter how he squirmed and stalled. "I suppose," he grunted, leaning in that she might reach him. When she did not move to place her hands upon his face—gods, this was the most embarrassing moment of his life—he took her wrists and guided her.

His mouth went dry, his gaze fixed upon her shining

countenance as deft, gentle fingers traveled over the ruins of what he'd once been told was a fine face. A handsome one, even, the sort that caught the eyes of the lasses even before they knew of his position as sole heir to his family's sizeable land holdings. He'd never much cared for talk of his physical beauty and had thus shrugged it off.

What a fool he'd been. He'd cared so little for the gift of a smooth, unscarred face. He'd taken for granted that his face would ever remain the same, or would at least until he was old and wrinkled.

If only he knew what she was thinking as she traveled those ruins. The knotty scar, rough and raised and bumpy. It started well above his hairline—he could cover it with hair there, at least. She found it, the expression on her lovely face never changing as she explored.

Until she winced, her hand trailing down until she was near his eye. He braced himself for her disgust. Instead, she whispered, "The blade came dangerously near your eye. Ye might have lost it."

"Aye," he muttered, his teeth clenched. As if he needed to be told of this.

She went on, examining his brows, his nose. His jaw, the planes of his cheeks. Her thumb ran over his lips and damned if he did not feel a spark of response deep inside. Not a muscle of her face twitched to reveal any reaction or even any opinion.

"Is your hair still brown as a chestnut?" she asked in a soft voice, sounding somewhat far away. She was elsewhere, concentrating on imagining him in her mind's eye.

"Aye."

"Your eyes? Grey?"

"Indeed."

She nodded, withdrawing her hands at last. He could breathe again, even as part of him regretted losing her touch. The lass had a gentle way about her, so unlike his rough, bitter self. She would wander the house in the darkness her eyes afforded her, making more of a point than ever to avoid him now that she knew what had been done to him. Her gentle nature would leave her quietl and fearful, avoiding him.

It would be a wonder if he ever managed to place a bairn in her belly—the act would likely terrify and disgust this sheltered, timid lass. There would never be joy, intimacy, pleasure.

He shook with rage at the terrible unfairness of it all.

"Ye had best be on yer way to bed," he decided, standing forcefully enough to nearly knock his chair backward. "We have quite a bit to do on the morrow."

Such as being wed.

6

———

If only she could see the fine wedding gown her father had made certain to secure. It felt so grand beneath her hands—silk, smooth and soft and rich. The finest thing she'd ever worn.

A pity the man she was about to wed would not appreciate it.

The thought of him of itself was enough to make her tremble. He was a fearsome man, to be certain, and she had the feeling he did not like her. Not merely the thought of her, the bride he'd been forced to wed, but her. As a person.

No one need tell Beitris as much. She knew it after spending no more than a few moments at his side. There was a way about him. He was angry, sullen, speaking in little more than grunts. There would be no quiet, peaceful evenings near the fire, speaking to each other in soft tones. Dreaming, planning. None of it.

He'd detested every moment of her touching his face,

seeing him. Yet marrying him would somehow have seemed even more of a horror if she'd done so without knowing precisely who she'd bound her life to.

He was just as terribly disfigured as he'd been described, she'd learned with a sinking heart which she'd endeavored to conceal. His right eyelid drooped, his brow split in two. The right corner of his mouth twisted upward thanks to scarring tugging at his skin and muscle. His fine, sharp jaw bore the worst of the rough, bumpy flesh.

Before his terrible injury, he must have made a handsome man—Elspeth had confirmed this, as well, remarking more than once on what a fine figure he'd once cut. More was the pity. Little wonder he was such a foreboding man.

He was, very much so. Foreboding to the point of frightening her. A terribly tall man, with wide shoulders against which brushed long, thick hair. Side whiskers grew wild on either side of his face—a pity they would not cover the worst of his wounds.

Little wonder the lasses in the household dreaded the sight of him, the sound of his approaching footfalls. She had already heard several of them whispering and warning each other of his approach before scurrying away. He was so terribly unpleasant, so bitter and hate-filled.

And he was to be her husband.

Her stomach turned, as it had turned every time the notion of wedding the man came to mind. Her heart fluttered, too, sickeningly. It left her weak, dizzy.

This was the beginning of the rest of her life, and she had nothing but fear of a bitter, angry husband to look forward to. Little wonder she lingered in the chambers prepared for her in advance of her arrival rather than opening the door and joining her father and Elspeth in the corridor.

"What ails ye?" Bruce muttered with his mouth near the door, likely of the belief she would be unable to hear him otherwise. "All are waiting in the great hall. Dinna cause me embarrassment, now."

"I shall be prepared in a moment," she assured him, as he would not cease pestering her until she offered response. How was she to manage this? How? Every day, so many days stringing together in an endless line. Nothing to look forward to. Nothing to hope for.

A single tear rolled down her cheek before she could stop it, and she quickly brushed it away. It would not do for her father to witness her tears, nor would it do Elspeth any good. The poor thing was worried enough, and angry enough.

Beitris stood, her legs shaking. There was nothing left to be done but to do the thing, to stand beside the man and pledge to be his faithful wife for as long as they should live. She was no wee lass, no child with dreams of love and romance and joy.

There were people for whom such things were possible, and people for whom they were not. She'd always known which of the two she was, had she not? Such dreams were not for one such as herself.

Had her father not reminded her time and again just how fortunate she was to have been accepted as a bride? No other man would have her. And while she'd railed against the notion of marriage for the sake of marriage in the past, she'd always known it was a wasted effort. There was no escaping the need to wed, for what other choice did she have?

A life lived entirely alone, without the protection of a man—father, brother, husband, it mattered not—was a life lived at the mercy of the world's cruelties, injustices, ignorance. She would have nothing.

A difficult truth, but true nonetheless. And Alasdair Macintyre was the only man who would have her.

This understanding carried her to the door, allowed her to pull it open. "Och, so 'tis alive, ye are," her father grumbled. "Ye have taken far too long. Ye shall be fortunate if yer intended will have ye now."

He would have her. She knew it. Normally, an apology would have tripped from her lips without her giving much thought to it. It seemed she'd spent most of her years apologizing for one thing or another. Today she would not apologize. Not today.

Instead, she took her father's arm and walked beside him down the wide, stone stairs. Fifteen in all, she'd counted them the night before. The heavy gown trailed behind her a bit, the sound of rustling silks mingling with Elspeth's barely-concealed weeping.

There were a great many candles burning in the great hall. Beitris could smell the fat melting and dripping, could just make out the glow from so many tiny flames combined. The lasses must have gathered nearly every nearby flower, and Beitris could not help but smile to herself at the scent of heather in the air. Had she not been thinking about the fields of heather upon reaching the farm?

"Ye ought to be proud, lass," Bruce muttered as he led her along. "Dinna disappoint me. Dinna disappoint yer new husband."

She did not say a word. She could not. If she opened her mouth, a sob would break loose and there would be no stopping herself from crumbling under the weight of it all.

They came to a stop, and Beitris recognized the scent of the man beside whom she'd taken her supper the evening prior. He smelled of earth, the leather of his saddle, fresh air. So he'd been out riding prior to their wedding, just as he'd gone out prior to their meeting. Perhaps he did this when there was a great trouble on his mind.

She held out her hand, waiting for his to join it. If only she could see him! If only there was some sense of how he felt, what he thought. She was at his mercy. Did he understand this?

If he did, he gave no indication as his hand touched hers. Rough, calloused, much larger. The hand of a powerful man, one strong enough to wield a sword in battle.

Would that he not use that hand to harm me, she prayed silently. The words of the ceremony made not a dent in her awareness, merely noise in the background of her thoughts. Her fears.

It had been a great deal of time since she'd prayed, really and truly. Prayer had so seldom resulted in anything worthwhile. There'd been times, especially during her youth, when Beitris had feared God deaf, as she was blind.

Why else would He so cruelly ignore her pleas?

Now, she prayed once more. *Please, let him be kind.* That was all. She dared not pray for love or affection. There were certain things she could not bring herself to hope for, as dashed hope was worst of all.

She was married before she knew it, married to a man who loomed over her like a mountain, all muscle and scarring and anger. Resentment toward her, toward the arrangement. Try as she might to stop herself, there was no helping the impulse to shrink away when he drew near.

7

———

After a month of marriage, Alasdair at last allowed himself to consider that his life might not be changed so drastically, after all.

He hardly saw the woman to whom he'd been wed, choosing to spend his days as he had prior to her arrival. Locked in his chambers, taking meals there, venturing out of doors in the wee hours of the morning and just before the sun set for walks and rides. He tended to become sore and stiff with inactivity, so taking great deals of fresh air was crucial.

Even in the rain, he could be seen exploring his lands, a hooded figure stalking along the banks of the creek.

If anyone were watching him, at any rate, which he imagined they did not. The household as a whole would rather pretend he did not exist, choosing to remove themselves from his path when they heard him approach. He'd taken to making a great deal of noise for that purpose, to give them time to hurry away.

The fewer people he saw during the course of a day, the better for all involved.

And not once had he set eyes upon the dark-haired, fearful little creature who now shared his name. Nor had he caught sight of her companion, thank the gods for that. He'd heard her voice, surely enough, shouting orders as if this were her family's ancestral home rather than his.

He might have taken offense to her ordering everyone about were it not for the sensible requests she made. Furnishings must be replaced precisely where they'd been before dusting or sweeping, for the mistress had committed to memory the exact location of each item. Elspeth shouted loud enough to all but bring the roof down, but those requests had been fewer as of late as the household became better inclined to consider Beitris as they went about their duties.

Truly, though he loathed the sound of the woman's voice, Elspeth's presence had done him a world of good. He need not venture from his chambers to see to his wife's needs, for they were already tended to. He need only continue living as he had before.

Alone, as he preferred it, now that his presence struck fear into the hearts of all with the misfortune of turning an eye upon him. It was better for all involved.

There was a great deal of work to be done in his study, the farm's accounts in serious disarray. It was clear that as his father's health had declined, so too had the amount of attention given the family's business dealings. Angus Macintyre had been a shrewd man, to be certain, the sort a man would regret ever attempting to cheat.

Word of his illness had spread, it was clear, for the costs of grain had risen most curiously. Overnight, it seemed. The steward had seen to the payment of these bills of sale, but as far as Alasdair knew there had been no questions raised.

Questions would be raised now, most certainly.

He made a great deal of noise as he left his bedchamber, clearing his throat and slamming the door behind him that anyone nearby might know he'd shown his hideous face. The corridor was clear, free of even a mouse, and he walked with a heavy tread down its length.

"Och, there ye be."

He stopped short at the top of the stairs when the now-familiar voice rang out. A good thing he had not started to descend, or else surprise might have sent him head-over-feet down their unforgiving length. Of all the people for him to cross paths with while he was already in a temper over the silver lost to unscrupulous merchants...

He turned on Elspeth, who marched toward him with the posture and expression of one marching into battle. She would make a fine soldier, at that.

"Aye, here I am," he barked before turning away from her and proceeding down the stairs. "What of it?"

She might have done him a good turn by seeing to his silent, invisible bride, but he was the master of the house and all surrounding it. She would do well to remember how he ought to be spoken to.

"Tis a miracle sent down from God himself, the fact that ye have shown yourself outside your chambers." Elspeth snorted, following him closely.

"Tis none of your affair, and I would thank ye to remember that," he grumbled, sweeping past the great hall on his way to the study. The lasses who happened to be in his path made haste to press themselves against the walls, their gaze cast downward.

"Perhaps 'tis none of my own, I shall grant ye, but 'tis verra much the affair of my mistress. Have ye forgotten? Ye are a wedded man."

He ducked to clear the door jamb while entering the study before whirling around to face her. "I am not aware of who gave the impression that ye are to speak to me as ye have done, but they were mistaken and so are ye. Dinna speak that way again."

She threw back her head hard enough to displace the linen cap she customarily wore, revealing red hair streaked with grey. "I shall speak to ye as I like, for I speak on behalf of my mistress. I serve her, not yourself. Ye dinna mean so much, even with all yer lands and yer wealth."

Damnable woman. There was a power to her, a strength, a nobility which caused him to shrivel inside. As a lad would shrivel upon being scolded by his mother or nurse. He was a grown man, a veteran of battle and the lord of the house, yet this woman somehow shrank him with a few angry words and an unflinching glare.

They'd already attracted far more attention than he felt comfortable with. "Inside," he growled, backing away that she might join him behind a closed door.

She did as he asked, deft fingers securing her cap in place once again. "Tis only of herself I am thinking," Elspeth murmured. "Ye have not considered her at all."

"And just how do ye wish me to consider her?" he muttered, stalking across the room toward the long table at which he worked. There were stacks of papers there, correspondence, bills of sale, ledgers. Let the woman see for herself how busy he was. How little affairs such as this mattered.

"Ye canna mean it." Elspeth gaped at him, standing on the other side of the table. "She is yer wife, and she has the makings of a fine one if only ye would give her the opportunity."

He scoffed openly, waving a dismissive hand. "Is this all ye have to say to me? For I dinna have the time. She is not mistreated or abused in any way. Have her meals been prepared for her? Has she every opportunity for new... gowns? Whatever 'tis she is in need of?" He had not the slightest notion of the particulars involved in dressing a woman.

"Aye, she has indeed," Elspeth admitted. "Though 'tis not enough. She lives in fear of ye, for she is a keen lass. Dinna allow her blindness to convince ye otherwise."

"Never would I make such a mistake," he vowed. He'd seen for himself how capable she was. And how keenly embarrassed by her father's drunken behavior the night before the wedding. She was a lass possessed of intelligence and determination. "Though I hardly ken how she might be afraid of me. I have given her no cause. I have not spoken to the lass—"

"Precisely!" The woman's face all but glowed in triumph. She had led him to exactly where she'd wished to go, and he'd followed all too willingly. "Ye have not spoken to her. Ye have not asked after her, not once since the day of the wedding. Ye have given her run of the house, 'tis true, but nothing else. Nothing of yerself. Ye are her husband, man! Why will ye not be a husband to her?"

"Tis none of your concern, and I would thank ye not to speak of such things. Tis no place of yours to question whether I have been a husband."

"We both know ye have not." Her voice was heavy with deeper meaning. The gall of the woman! To question him, to challenge him, to stand before him and reference the fact that he had not consummated his marriage.

As if he could. As if the notion of forcing himself upon a blind, weeping lass did not make him wish he'd died upon the field of battle. There were men who would, naturally, men who would care nothing for how the lass felt. Who would take her because it was their right, because she was theirs to be taken.

He could not imagine such cruelty, could not bring himself to envision it.

"How dare ye?" he whispered, fists clenched in rage. "Remove yourself from my presence at once, or else ye shall return to Bruce Boyd or send ye die in the road for all that it matters to me."

"Och, ye canna frighten me as ye do the others about the place," she scoffed. "And I would sooner cut off my own head than I would abandon my Beitris, so ye might just as well leave off all such thoughts of turning me away."

He had to admire her, if grudgingly. Her fierce devotion was a rare thing.

Though she did not admire him. That much was clear. In fact, she sneered openly. "Ye believe yerself to be so fearsome, and ye believe ye command respect simply because ye happened to be born to Angus Macintyre. I canna respect ye, not after ye have unfairly judged my mistress."

His impulse was to bellow, to shout at the top of his lungs, to shout at her to leave him. Once he'd finished, she would beg to be allowed to abandon her beloved Beitris. He'd make life a misery for this overly-opinionated, screeching harpy.

Perhaps his better nature was able to overcome this impulse, for he maintained his composure long enough to ask, "How have I done so?"

"Ye assume her to be useless, 'tis how," she spat. "As if she were nothing more than an animal to be placed in a pen. Her needs might be seen to, but what else is there? Dinna ye imagine her to have feelings? Thoughts? Dinna ye imagine she might be lonely?"

"She has ye."

"I canna be all." Elspeth lowered her voice, meeting his gaze squarely. "She asks not for love. My lass is too wise to believe such a thing possible. What she requires is companionship, or at least the sense that she has not been forgotten and disregarded. She has been disregarded her entire life, passed by, overlooked simply because she canna see. Allow me to assure ye, she sees a great deal more than either ye or myself are capable of."

He sat back, at a loss now. It was not often a woman was able to talk her way around him, but not often had he been as deeply wrong as he was in his handling of Beitris. "Aye. I dinna doubt it," he murmured, gazing past her, seeing how wrong he'd been.

There was nothing else to be done about this, it seemed, for the woman would not give him a moment's peace until he agreed. "Do me the favor of asking my wife if she would be inclined to ride with me later today," he muttered, feeling clumsy and foolish. "Tis my custom to walk or ride about prior to taking the evening meal. I would... enjoy her companionship."

What did he expect? That she would weep and offer thanks? Unlikely. "See to it she enjoys yours," Elspeth warned before storming from the room, slamming the door behind her.

To think. The servants ran from him, when it ought to be Elspeth who struck fear in their hearts.

8

———

"Ye need not hold my reins," Beitris insisted for at least the third time since they'd started out. "I can ride, and the mare sees for me."

"Does my wishing to see to your safety cause you offense?" Alasdair asked.

It seemed a sincere question, asked in a voice far softer than she'd heard from him before then. "It does not," she decided. "Ye dinna offend me."

"Does it cause discomfort, my riding so near yourself?"

If only her skin would not flush at the question, as if he sensed her discomfort. Who would blame her? He'd spoken not a word to her since the day of their being wed, and now he wished them to ride together.

She was unaccustomed to him because of this. His physical nearness was enough to take her breath away—after all, the reins were but so long, and he insisted on keeping them in his hand. He rode quite near, their legs brushing now and again.

Yet he had not been cruel, and in fact had spoken gently since meeting her in the stables. As though he were a different man entirely. Perhaps his heart had changed toward her.

He waited for her response. "Nay," she decided. "It does not."

"Then, if 'tis the same to ye, I would prefer to keep hold of the reins. Until ye are better accustomed to the terrain, that is," Alasdair added. "I have no doubt ye are capable."

"Truly?" she whispered, then wished she had not. There was entirely too much hope in that whisper, and she did not wish for him to hear it. Was it not enough that she endured being shunned for the first month of marriage?

"Truly," he assured her with a smile in his voice. She heard warmth, as well, something she'd not heard during their brief time together before now. "Ye have managed to learn your way about verra well, so I have heard. Ye require little assistance and would always rather do things on your own."

"This is true," she agreed.

"Take care with that, I warn ye. There are times when accepting assistance is necessary. T'would be a pity if ye came to harm because ye were too stubborn to ask for help."

"I am not stubborn." She turned her face toward his, lifting it slightly to make up for the difference in their heights. "I will not be called stubborn."

"Forgive me," he murmured, still smiling in his voice. "I didna intend to offend ye. I do wish ye would heed my advice, just the same."

"Ye are suddenly concerned for my welfare?"

Perhaps she ought not have said it. His sharp intake of breath spoke to how she'd surprised him. "I was not warned of your sharp tongue," he murmured.

"Tis a weakness, to be certain," she breathed by way of apology.

"Nothing less than what I deserve. I have not been the husband I ought to be."

They rode in silence for many long, silent minutes. Beitris could not help but wonder if he would become angry, as he'd been these long weeks. It seemed his nature to be short-tempered, furious at all times. She ought not to have allowed her sharp tongue to get away from her.

Water flowed somewhere close by, to her left. "Is there a stream near?" she asked in a soft voice, wishing to ease any anger he felt toward her. Perhaps if they discussed something else, something which had nothing to do with the two of them, any anger would ease.

"Aye, there is," he uttered. It was not a grunt, which she supposed was a good sign.

"Do ye often ride near the stream?"

"When possible, aye. I spent a great deal of time here before..." He stopped himself, and she knew better than to press further.

"Might ye... describe it to me?" she asked with her heart in her throat. "So I might see it?"

He cleared his throat. She sensed his discomfort and asked herself whether she'd made a dreadful mistake. Perhaps this was too much, too quickly. They'd never been alone together until this day.

"The stream is a bit swollen thanks to the rain of these last several days," Alasdair began in a tight voice, though that was better than his usual harsh tone. "It overflows the banks on either side. The spruce grows thick here."

"Aye, I can smell it," she said with a smile.

"Do ye hear the squirrels and hares?"

"I do. The squirrels run up and down the trunks, frolicking among themselves."

He chuckled. It was a nice sound, comforting. "They are enjoying a fine day. Tis ever the way of it after a heavy rain."

"Indeed," she agreed.

"There is one tree which sits apart from the others." He spoke slowly now, choosing his words with care. "Tis no longer living. I... often sat beneath it as a lad."

"Did ye, then?" She grinned, turning toward him as their mounts continued a slow, steady pace. "To sulk?"

His laughter was so fine, rich and deep. It rang out like music on the warm, fresh air and lightened her heart considerably. "Perhaps more often than not," he admitted. "To think, most of all. Where none would find me."

"I often wished for such a secret place," she admitted. "But I could not go on my own, not any great distance."

"Och, 'tis sorry I am for that." He sighed. "Every lad and lass ought to be able to escape their elders."

He was so different here, away from the house and all

who were able to see his face. Softer, kinder, gentler. She was no longer afraid of him. If only he could behave in such a manner always.

"If ye could escape to this secret place now, what would ye think of?" she ventured. Why not? She did long to know him better, that she might no longer dread the notion of crossing his path. He was a man, not a monster of nightmare. A man who'd once escaped to the creek and his secret tree when he wished to be alone.

"I would curse myself for having been such a poor example of a husband," he admitted with a sigh. "Ye canna ken how it pains me to admit it, Beitris."

He'd never used her name before, had he? It warmed her all over to hear it, though she could not quite understand why.

"Ye must hate me terribly," he muttered. "None would blame ye, mind."

"I dinna hate ye," she assured him with a smile. "For I dinna ken what to expect from a husband. My mam went on to her reward long ago. I have no memory of her, or of the manner in which she and my father behaved together."

"My mam passed on while birthing me," he explained, though she knew it well. "And my father... he was a great man, a mighty man. A brave warrior in his day. He taught me many things. How to be a man, how to be strong. But not how to act as a husband. I know not the first thing about being a husband."

She knew she ought not laugh, but there was no

helping it. "I know not how to be a wife! It seems we are well-matched, after all."

His laughter mingled with hers, rising above the sound of rushing creek waters. "What are we to do, then?" he asked once they'd calmed themselves.

"I could not say," she confessed, shrugging. "This is fine, though. Perhaps we might ride more. And walk. I would love to see the lands, so long as ye are willing to describe them."

"I am, at that," he guaranteed her with a smile in his voice. "Whenever ye like."

9

———

"Ye are certain of this?"

Alasdair stared at the man before him, one with whom he was familiar. One who'd earned his trust on the field of battle. "Aye. I have received word from several of the men in the village. There is no doubt. Ye ken well how men talk once they've had their fill of ale."

"Englishi agents." The words fell like iron weights which somehow landed on his chest and made it difficult to breathe. "How long has it been since they've arrived?"

"I canna say." Colin Ramsey stood with one hand fixed around the hilt of his sword. As sheriff of the surrounding area, it was his duty to maintain order. As such, he and his men routinely patrolled the village and the farms bordering it, listening to local gossip and keeping watch for threats.

A threat had arrived, to be certain.

"They are searching for those of us who fought with

Charlie, then," Alasdair mused. Bonnie Prince Charles and his damnable war. A war which had left Alasdair disfigured, which had left many men and lads dead or limbless, had left wives and bairns weeping and alone.

It was not enough for the English to stamp down the rebellious Jacobites. They would not be satisfied until they killed every last man who'd dared fight against them. Though the battle was long over, the danger was not yet past.

Cruel, heartless beasts.

"I felt it best to make ye aware of this," Colin murmured, his dark eyes hard and narrowed. "As I am acting sheriff of the region, they canna do much to me without alerting others to their scheme. Too many people would get word of it, and they canna have that."

"I see," Alasdair murmured, his mood darkening by the moment.

Colin lowered his gaze to his sword. "It might be wise for any who fought against the English to take care in the coming days. To avoid notice whenever possible. Especially anyone with..." He lifted a hand, waving it vaguely before his face. "Identifying marks."

"Aye," Alasdair agreed. "Perhaps t'would be wise for anyone fitting that description to remain away from the village."

"Aye. I suspected ye would agree with me. I'd best be on my way." Colin was a man of few words, which may have been why the two of them had gotten on well as soldiers.

The damned English. Was it not enough they'd

defeated man such as himself, to say nothing of so many others? He swept an arm over the table, sending papers and candles scattering over the floor.

That wasn't enough. The table itself went next, crashing against the stone beneath it loudly enough to make him flinch. Yet it did nothing to soothe the sense of hopeless anger which threatened to consume him.

"What have ye done here?" Elspeth peered into the study, aghast at the destruction.

"Leave me be," he warned, turning his back to her, pounding the side of one fist against the wall near the window.

"Why have ye done it?"

"Have ye lost use of your hearing?" he demanded. "I ordered ye to leave me be!"

"I dinna accept orders from ye." He heard her enter the room, heard her mutter to herself as she sank to her knees and shuffled papers into stacks. "What led ye to this? Behaving as a bairn might when he's not allowed his way. I dinna ken why the lasses and even the lads are frightened of ye. Ye are little better than a child."

He snapped around, prepared to shout at the woman until she dissolved in tears.

Yet another thought entered his mind, wedging itself between his rage and his good sense and calming his flared temper. "Ye must keep closer watch on Beitris than ever."

Elspeth cast a suspicious glance his way, still kneeling in the middle of the destruction he'd created. "Why, then? Do ye intend to repeat this in her chambers?"

"Listen to me." He crouched before her, forcing himself to ignore the disdain so evident in her expression. "We must take care with her. There are English agents in the village, seeking men who fought against them. Did ye catch sight of the sheriff? He paid a call."

"Aye, I did at that," she whispered, sitting back on her heels, the papers forgotten.

"He came to issue a warning. I am far too easily recognized. I must remain hidden when possible, or else face capture."

"Why would they wish to capture ye?"

"Why would they wish to capture anyone?" he asked, allowing her to see and hear his dismay. "But they have it in mind. Tis a blessing Colin was able to warn me. We must keep watch on Beitris, more closely than ever. I am certain that by now, word has spread of my wedding a blind lass. There could be men in the woods, or even trespassing on our land. We canna allow her to fall into their clutches."

The most surprising thing happened then. For the first time since they'd met—it had been more than two months now—Elspeth's face softened in his presence. Rather than glaring at him, or scowling, or looking him up and down as if he were something unpleasant, she nearly smiled while tears welled in her eyes.

Rather than pretending he did not understand why she looked this way, he made certain to add, "We canna tell her of this. She would worry needlessly if she knew."

"Of course," Elspeth whispered. Suddenly, they were confidants, working together to ensure Beitris's safety and sense of comfort. "And ye must take great care. Dinna risk yourself."

"I assure ye," he murmured as he stood. "Beitris would be cared for in the event of my... If anything were to occur."

She stood as well, thrusting a sheaf of parchment at him. "If ye believe she would only fret over her being provided for after the pair of ye have spent each morning and evening wandering together, I dinna have anything more to say."

What did that mean? She offered no explanation, leaving him to ponder this along with everything else Colin's warning had brought to mind.

10

"Why are ye so terribly worried?" Beitris laughed, walking with her hand on Elspeth's arm as they made their way through the village. It was a busy morning, as ever, leaving her no choice but to remain close or risk becoming hopelessly turned around—if she was not run down by a team of horses or oxen.

"Am I terribly worried?" Elspeth asked with a soft, nervous laugh, pulling Beitris away from a group of shouting men walking in the other direction.

"Aye, ye are at that. I hear it in your voice, or have ye forgotten?"

"I have not forgotten. Tis merely that Alasdair—"

She let out a frustrated grunt. "Dinna speak to me of my husband. He is entirely too protective of my safety, when there is no call to be. He ought to ken by now how capable I am of something as simple as walking to the village and gathering food for the cook."

It was enough to make her want to scream—in fact, she'd once buried her face in her pillow and done just that after being scolded by her good husband. He felt her unable to walk to the creek on her own, though she'd committed to memory the number of steps it took to reach the banks and had traveled the path more times than she could count.

"He cares a great deal for your safety," Elspeth crooned. "Dinna take it hard."

Beitris scoffed. "Ye sound a great deal like my longtime companion, yet the words ye speak sound nothing like what Elspeth would say in regard to my husband."

"Ye take me wrong."

"Nay, I dinna believe I do." She came to a stop, forcing Elspeth to do the same. Villagers moved around them, going about their daily affairs with little care for the pair of women speaking closely. "What has happened? Ye have softened toward him. I have known it for many days, though I've thought better of speaking of it."

Elspeth snickered. "What of it? Time has altered my view of the man. He is not as heartless as I first imagined. I am many things, Beitris, but I am not unreasonable."

Beitris kept her thoughts on this to herself, knowing better than to offer a challenge no matter how warranted. Elspeth was the sort of woman whose opinion could not be swayed.

They continued, intent on visiting the butchery for

sausages. "Alasdair enjoys sausages for supper," was Beitris's reason for wishing to go out of their way.

"Och, and ye care so verra much for what he enjoys?" Elspeth asked.

"Are ye laughing at me?"

"Nay, not at all. I find it a matter of interest, is all. How ye wish to make him happy."

"He is my husband." She left it there, for there was no further explanation to be offered. Why would she not wish to do little things for him, to prove she held him in her thoughts as she went about her day? They'd agreed during that first ride, when they'd admitted to having no notion of how to behave as husband and wife, to be as kind and thoughtful as possible.

The butchery shop was dreadfully crowded—Beitris heard the many voices coming from inside before they'd reached the threshold. "Perhaps we'd better not," she suggested, disappointed at her plan being foiled. "We might return another time."

"I might go inside, if ye would be so good as to wait," Elspeth suggested.

"Ye need not—"

"Nay," Elspeth laughed. "Ye wish to please your husband, and I would not wish to see ye unable to do so. If there are too many inside for ye to be comfortable, wait here. I shall not be long."

Beitris was content to wait out of doors, where she might at least breathe fresh air. There were so many different aromas in the air. Bread, pies. Horses, oxen, pigs being driven down the road. Some might wrinkle their noses at the scent, but she found it invigorating. This was how she became aware of her surroundings. She could all but see it in front of her, in fact, as if her eyesight had not failed at all.

If only Alasdair were there to describe it, the entire scene might be clearer. He had a way of describing their surroundings which brought the world to life. She would never have imagined it coming from a man such as himself, that he would take the time and care to ensure she had a clear understanding of everything around them.

"He wears a scar along the side of his face."

Her head snapped up, turning her ear in the direction of this deep, unfamiliar voice. There was a chance the man did not speak of Alasdair—he was not the only man in Scotland with a scar—but the mention of it was bound to make her sit up a bit straighter and pay attention.

"Yes, everyone is aware of the severity of his wounds," a second man replied. "His hideous countenance is legend." They were English, these men, which left her gritting her teeth. She possessed no great love for the English, any more than any of her kinsmen.

To know a English soldier had so wounded Alasdair merely added to that hatred.

The man continued. "He is an enemy of the crown. The man who reported him to the magistrate shall collect a large bounty, I'm sure. And they who turn him in shall collect a sum, as well." A price on his head? Why? What had he done? Who had she bound her life to?

"He is known to visit the village now and then." The man grunted. They stood nearby, perhaps outside the baker's. "It is only a matter of time before we find him. And when we do..."

"What is the command?" the second man asked. Yes. What was the command? Beitris's fingers nearly tore through the woven basket she held in her lap. "Are we to bring him before the magistrate?"

"Not while he breathes—he would fight too fiercely," the first man laughed.

"How are we to manage it?"

The first man scoffed. "A simple matter, that. The cur will be killed on sight."

Beitris clutched her basket tighter than ever, her heart in her throat. She could scarcely breathe. They wished to kill him! Someone had put a price on his head, and he would die because of it.

She could not simply sit and wait for them to find him. Every moment might be a moment wasted. What if Alasdair decided to ride to the village that very day? Her stomach churned at the idea. She would lose him. He would die and someone would collect a reward as if he meant nothing more than a bag of silver.

Rising on shaking legs, Beitris took pains to appear unaffected. She turned in the direction from which she and Elspeth had come and began to walk. How she intended to find her way home was not something she could trouble her head over just then. She simply had to be on her way. Elspeth could find and catch her, no doubt.

And she did before long, gasping for air upon reaching Beitris's side. "What have ye taken into yer head, lass?" Elspeth gasped, pulling her to a stop. "Walking alone? Ye would never find yer way!"

"Was I moving in the correct direction?"

"...aye," the older woman admitted, still breathless. "What are ye on about then?"

"Come," Beitris whispered, taking her companion's arm. "We must make haste. It might already be too late. If he rides out today—"

"Alasdair?"

Beitris held a finger to her lips. "Dinna speak his name until we are alone. Is anyone following us?"

"Following?"

"Aye!" she snapped. Why was it so difficult to make the woman understand? "Is there anyone, any man, behind us?"

"Nay, not following, in any case."

She could breathe a bit easier. "I overheard men speaking of him. Dinna speak his name," she warned again. "There is a price on his head. He is to be killed on sight."

"He never is!" Elspeth gasped, clutching Beitris's hand. "Och, 'tis dreadful! He said nothing of being killed!"

"He has spoken to ye of this?" Beitris demanded, trembling, her feet all but flying over the now-familiar ground between the village and the farm.

"Aye," Elspeth admitted. "A fortnight ago. The sheriff warned there were English agents in the village, searching for Scottish soldiers."

"One soldier in particular," Beitris spat in disgust. "Someone brought his name to the magistrate, and the man wishes him dead."

"Do ye know why?"

"I did not wait to hear anything more. I had to—that is, I needed—"

"Ye need not explain," Elspeth assured her, patting her hand. "Tis a blessing I finished at the butchery when I did. Come. Let us make haste. Yer husband would not ride to the village, not now. Not while he is aware of the danger."

Beitris could only hope that Elspeth was correct. It was rare that she spoke an untruth. But how was she to know? Was she merely offering empty words to sooth Beitris's troubled mind?

The thought of Alasdair being killed, offered up for a reward. It brought tears to her eyes, left an ache in her chest which refused to be soothed.

In spite of the manner in which they'd met, and in spite of how long it had taken them to start learning about each other, there was little doubt that Alasdair Macintyre had begun to work his way into her affections. He was still rather coarse at times, still easily angered, but at his core he was a good, decent man who'd been sorely mistreated.

And he was hers, and she could not lose him.

11

———

"Where is my wife?" Alasdair demanded, asking the question of no one in particular as he strode down the corridor. There were normally at least five or six lasses at work in the household at once, including the cook, yet he'd seen none of them that morning.

For a moment, he thought none of them would answer him, that they were hiding. Had he frightened them that much, then? So badly they were afraid to even speak when spoken to?

Finally, he met up with the cook at the foot of the stairs. "The mistress walked to the village and offered to fetch items for our supper," she explained. A woman of advanced years, she was not so easily intimidated.

Yet she backed away with a look of horror on her lined face when his fists clenched in frustration. "With Elspeth, I imagine?" he growled.

The woman was too frightened to speak, choosing to nod instead before hurrying to the kitchen. It was ridiculous, the way they ran from him. As though he were a monster. Had he ever harmed them? Had he ever even come close?

No, and certainly none of them had run from him in earlier times. Better times. After these many months, he still found the members of his household shrinking away from his mangled countenance.

He pushed this from his mind, as he tried to do more often as of late. There was no sense in reminding himself of the way things used to be, of how his life had once been lived. How much better it might have been had he never fought in that useless, wasteful war.

After all, there was no telling whether some other tragedy would not have befallen him. He might've been thrown from his horse, trampled, gored by a bore. Such calamities occurred every day.

Besides, there was no sense in turning his mind toward anything other than the present moment, as his life was no longer only his own. His leadership meant security for his entire household, for the farm itself.

And for his wife, whose absence from the house he felt most keenly. She was not present for their morning ride. He had not known until just then, that very morning, that he'd come to look forward to those times together. Quiet times, rides during which neither of them needed to speak. There was a sense of contentment at simply being with someone else, at no longer being alone.

No. Not with someone else. With her.

Strange, but the act of describing their surroundings, as a painter would use brushstrokes to craft an image, added to his appreciation for the farm he had already loved so well. It sounded daft, and he knew it, but he saw things more clearly thanks to her.

Though he would rather bite off his own tongue than ever give voice to these thoughts. There were certain things a man did not speak of, especially if he wished to be respected.

Although, in his heart, he thought she might understand. Of all people, she would understand.

Little did it matter, as she was in the village. It had been a fortnight since his visit from Colin, since he'd confessed to Elspeth the danger he was in—and Beitris, besides. He did not doubt the woman would risk her life to save her charge, if need be.

Though of course, he would prefer if such an occasion would not arise.

What was he to do, then? He went to his study, pacing for several minutes and rubbing his hands together. What had he done at one time, before Beitris's arrival? Rather, before they began spending time together? Back when he had so deeply valued his solitude. Had there been a time when he'd resented her for destroying that blessed loneliness?

Now, he cursed her for being away when he wished to see her.

He would hunt. It had been far too long since he'd

hunted in the woods just bordering the creek. They would be full by now, with deer, hare, squirrel. There would be no shortage of opportunity.

Besides, it was a sight better than taking his anger out upon anyone beneath his roof.

It did not take long for him to prepare, as he had already been prepared for a morning spent in the out of doors. All that was needed were his bow and a quiver of bolts. A brisk hike into the woods would clear his head and remove the tightness from his chest.

Still, he was not satisfied, even after felling a young buck within an hour of wandering the wood. There was no joy in the kill—in fact, upon reflection, he realized there was little joy in killing any creature after what he'd seen the past spring. That spring, and the months before. The entire year in which he'd been absent from his ancestral home.

It would be one matter if there was not far more than enough game in the smokehouse and the kitchen. This was not hunting for sustenance. This was hunting for sport, and his heart was no longer in it. What had become of him?

His ears pricked up at the sound of snapping twigs not far from where he crouched beside the bleeding buck. It would be a large animal from the sounds of it charging through the brush. Another buck? Perhaps a doe? No, they would have fled at the scent of blood, unwilling to leave themselves vulnerable to his arrow.

What, then? The only creature foolish enough to venture so near the site of a fresh kill was man.

He had only just stood and prepared a fresh bolt when

the men in question revealed themselves. Two of them, both dressed roughly, unkempt and ragged.

And smiling broadly, as though they had discovered prize game before them.

All at once, he understood they had. These were not mere strangers, passersby in the woods. They were not even thieves—and he was suddenly aware that for all their filth, they were not as they appeared to be. They were in disguise, hoping to hide what they truly were. Mercenaries. English.

All of this went by in an instant, no longer than the time it took to blink an eye. A moment later, sunlight glinted off the metal barrel of a flintlock an instant before the man aiming it pulled the trigger.

Alasdair was not fast enough. While the ball might have struck his heart if he had not jumped aside, it did lodge itself in his left shoulder. He cried out in pain and surprise, blood spurting from the wound in an instant.

"You are coming with us," the second man declared, charging at him while the first man prepared for another shot. There was no time to think, not even any time to doubt whether it was a wise decision to use his wounded shoulder. It was either raise the bow or be captured. Or worse.

The muscles in his ruined shoulder screamed as he pulled back the bolt and let it fly, striking the charging attacker in the upper thigh. He fell, clutching his wounded leg, bellowing like a wounded animal.

There was no time to prepare another bolt, as the

armed man took another shot. Fire spread through Alistair's right side. He pressed a hand to the wound, blood pouring over his fingers, and for an instant he may as well have been on the field of battle once again.

Sheer fury washed over him, blurring his vision as rage took over for sensibility. This was the sort of frenzy a man experienced in battle, when all of life boiled down to a single choice. Kill or be killed.

And so, bleeding and in terrible pain, Alistair gouged at the man's eyes, clawing his face and throat as they tangled. He might have been scarred, he might have been bleeding heavily in two places, but no man in possession of his senses would dare underestimate him.

Finally, one powerful blow to the side of the attacker's head left him dropping to the ground, unconscious. The wounded man, bolt still sticking out from his thigh, attempted to crawl deeper into the woods.

Alistair took this opportunity to flee, dragging himself from the woods, moving from one tree to the next. He would lean against them for a moment, each in turn, willing himself the strength to continue to the trunk up ahead.

Where had they come from? Had they been awaiting him all that time? Or had they been on their way to the farm? Indeed, there was no reason for them to expect his presence—he rarely hunted, rarely ventured into the dense woods at all now that most of his outdoor ventures involved his sightless wife.

Precious blood spilled upon the ground, splashing and

dripping with each plodding step. Terrible memories flashed before him, mingling with the present until it was difficult to tell one from the other. Staggering among the bodies, the limbs which had been cut free. The stench of blood, both his own and that of so many others, made him ill, his stomach threatening to let loose its contents.

By the time he staggered into the courtyard, the world was blurring before his eyes. He grunted with each step, dragging himself, determined that none who witnessed this would see him fall.

He might have wept with relief at the site of his bride rushing down the stairs from her chambers. "Beitris," he groaned as his legs threatened to go out from beneath him.

"What has happened?" she asked, running one hand along the wall as she descended.

"I must go to my chambers," he grunted, hearing the weakness in his voice. She heard it, as well, and like as not smelled the blood which had soaked into his tunic, his trousers.

Somewhere in the back of his mind, he heard Beitris calling for help as she guided him up the stairs. To think, a blind lass guided him. Yet she knew the way, knew it is if she could see all before her.

"What happened?" she whispered as she assisted him down the corridor. For one so slight, she possessed a great deal of strength, allowing him to lean against her as his strength failed.

"Two men," he grunted, teeth clenched against the pain

which burned anew with each step. "Ne'er had I seen them before."

"The men sent to kill ye?" she whispered feverishly as she helped him onto his bed. He groaned terribly, hating his weakness but knowing there was no hope. His side was on fire, his shoulder pained to the point of uselessness.

Surprise cut through the pain, at least for a moment. "Ye know that?" he demanded. "How?"

"I heard word of it in the village," she admitted, nimble fingers moving over his shoulder. "Ye must remove the tunic. Where is Elspeth?" she asked, raising her voice.

"Here," Elspeth nearly barked as she entered the room with steaming bowl of water, linen towels draped over one arm.

"I shall need your assistance," Beitris informed her, her hands now moving over Alasdair's side. He grimaced, grunting every bit of profanity he knew, and her brow furrowed.

Yet it was not due to his use of language, he learned. "Forgive me," she whispered. "I dinna wish to bring you pain."

"Tis none of your doing," he assured her through gritted teeth, marveling at how capable she was. "Ye need not apologize."

Elspeth soaked a towel in steaming water, handing another, dry towel to Beitris. "Spread this out beside him," she advised. "To soak up the blood."

"I know not how much more I can stand to lose," he admitted with a faint laugh, swaying in place. Indeed, the world was beginning to fade before him, everything turning dark.

A sharp slap sent his head reeling backward, bringing the world back to him. "Forgive me," Beitris murmured, shaking out the hand she'd used before returning her attention to cleansing the wound in his shoulder. "But ye must tell me. Where are the men? What became of them?"

"One crawled away with my bolt sticking out from his leg," he whispered, weaker with each breath he took. "The other I left there, after striking him about the head."

"We must remove the lead from his wounds," Elspeth fretted. "He will be poisoned by it."

"I'm aware of this," Beitris assured her in calm, low voice. She then placed a palm against his cheek, where she had just struck him. "Ye have nothing to fear."

If only that were true. For all he could imagine in those final moments of wakefulness was losing the wondrous creature who'd found a way past his hideous scars, who saw the man beneath them more surely then anyone with perfect eyesight ever could.

He covered her hand with his own, blood-covered as it was, before descending into darkness.

12

———

Beitris dragged an arm over her forehead, wiping away sweat which had beaded there during the delicate task of removing lead shot from her husband's shoulder. With him unconscious, she'd used her fingers to work through the delicate tissue while grinding her teeth together hard enough to hurt.

The second ball had gone through his side, exiting from behind, and Elspeth had burned the wounds closed after cleansing them again.

Though she knew her husband was unaware of this, far away in some dark, painless place, tears had welled in Beitris's eyes when the sound of his sizzling flesh reached her ears. Even now, knowing he was resting and out of danger for the moment, she could scarcely breathe for the fear.

What if the shot had pierced his heart? Or his head? What if he'd fallen dead on the spot?

Someone would be much richer for it, no doubt. Bile rose in her throat when she imagined this person, the one who'd turned Alasdair's name over to the magistrate. Only the lowest sort of person would benefit from the murder of another.

His breathing was steady, quiet, and she was glad of this. She sat beside him, the chair drawn up close to the bed. Elspeth had urged her to leave him for the moment, to wash and refresh herself. But Beitris could not leave him.

She also could not allow him to remain in the house, and she knew it. What if those men were to return? What if they were to bring the magistrate along with them? Certainly, they would not rest until Alasdair was captured. Not now, not when he had bested them.

Elspeth's rapid footfalls foretold her approach. When she entered the room, Beitris whispered, "He canna remain here."

Elspeth placed a bowl in Beitris's lap. "Ye must eat." The scent of stew filled the air, reminding Beitris she had not eaten since dawn.

Certainly, however, she had not felt the absence of food. Not when Alasdair might be dying. Even now, with a delectable aroma making her mouth water, she could hardly bring herself to imagine placing so much as a bite in her mouth. "We must move him," she insisted, whispering in case he were to regain consciousness and overhear. "What if they are to return? We canna allow him to be captured."

Elspeth sighed. "Yes, I had considered this while in the

kitchen. T'would be dangerous for ye if he were to be discovered here."

Beitris scoffed. "Tis not for myself that I fear."

"I know it well," Elspeth assured her. "But I fear for ye. And I suspect yer husband would feel the same. He would not wish for ye to be endangered for his sake."

A strange warmth spread through her chest, and perhaps there would be time in the future to consider why that warmth existed. Now, there was little time to lose.

"There must be somewhere for him to hide," Beitris mused. "Somewhere they canna find him. But where?"

"Ye have learned more of the farm and the surrounding lands than I have, certainly," Elspeth pointed out. "Is there nowhere he might be concealed?"

"There is a cave." Beitris's head snapped up, envisioning the cave in her mind's eye. "He has described it to me, though we never ventured that far. Tis just beneath the hills at the northern end of the family's lands, where the creek joins with the river which borders the eastern edge."

"The pair of ye have done quite a bit of exploring, have ye now?"

"Tis my land, as well," Beitris reminded her. "As a Macintyre, I must be aware of the lands entrusted to my husband."

"I would never question ye," Elspeth assured her.

Beitris pushed this aside. There was no time for such petty arguing. "Perhaps we might hide him there," she decided. "I doubt many others are aware of the cave's presence. From what he described, the mouth is half-hidden by spruce and overgrowth."

"How would the pair of us manage to take him there? Such a large man as himself will not be easily moved."

Yes, this was a concern. "We may have to make him ride. Though I doubt either of us is strong enough to help him into the saddle."

"Aye, and what if he falls from the saddle? He has lost such a great deal of blood."

"We might load him into the wagon, then." Yes, this was a wise decision. If he were to fall unconscious again, it would not result in greater injury. "I will need ye to watch for the cave."

"As if I would allow ye to go on your own," Elspeth scoffed. "Go to yer chambers and change into a clean dress. I must insist. Wash yer hands and face, as well. If any were to see us driving the wagon, they would question yer appearance."

Naturally, Elspeth made a good point. Beitris dashed down the corridor, listening for any voices in passing. Only when she'd reached her chambers did she recall this was the day when most of the household went to the village, to visit friends or family. No one would return until after supper except the cook, who'd been busy with her work all day. It was a blessing, to be sure. The fewer people aware of this, the better for all.

She washed quickly, scrubbing beneath her nails to remove any traces of blood, then changed out of her ruined dress. She even went so far as to unwind her braid, brushing her hair back and braiding it again. After all, Elspeth had foreseen a possible difficulty: if anyone were to come upon them, they would ask why she was disheveled. Especially if they'd already gotten word of a skirmish in the wood.

Alasdair was awake, at least partly, when she returned to his chambers. "The cave is an inspired notion," he whispered. The sound of his voice was enough to inspire hope that his recovery would be swift—he was conscious, he was aware of his surroundings and capable of understanding their plan.

Yet she could not cease fretting for him. "Save your strength," she was quick to reply. "Ye shall need to rest quite a bit if ye are to heal, and as I canna be at the cave with ye at all times, ye shall need to care for yourself now and again."

"I ken too well," he chuckled without humor. "Ye have both done marvelously well. Better than I could hope to do on my own."

"Show me the man strong enough to remove lead shot from his own shoulder," Elspeth snickered. "Ye did admirably, if I do say so. Bringing yerself here, that is. Many a man would have given up."

Were Beitris's ears deceiving her? She'd never heard Elspeth use such a soft, admiring tone with Alasdair. It was far likelier that she'd curse him or criticize.

"I assume t'was yourself who burned the wounds closed?" he asked, pain heavy in his voice. "Ye did well. I thank ye."

Truly, this was the strangest day. Beitris merely shook her head while gathering a clean tunic and trousers, stockings and boots for Alasdair. Fresh linen bandages, blankets... what else might he need? "Elspeth, see to fetching food. Dinna allow the cook to know what ye are about."

"I will." She hurried from the room, leaving Beitris alone with her husband. In his bedchamber, while he was awake and aware. Why did this matter in the slightest? She could not say, even to herself. It seemed there was no calming the heat in her cheeks.

"Ye must dress as best ye can," she murmured.

"I... may be in need of assistance," he replied in a choked voice. Like as not, the pain was unbearable. Not only had he been twice shot, but his burns had only just been bandaged.

"I shall do what I might." She shook out the tunic and slid one sleeve over his uninjured arm before guiding the wounded arm through. His sharp intake of breath, followed by a groan, brought her up short. "Forgive me."

"Dinna ask for forgiveness, lass. I owe ye my life."

"If only I might have warned ye to remain indoors, but we were not quick enough in returning from the village. I knew not where ye might have gone." She turned her face away that he might not spy the tears filling her eyes at the memory of her desperation. How certain she'd been that he'd already met with danger.

And how correct she'd been, as well.

It was not easy, ignoring the muscles of his arms and shoulders, his chest and back as she helped him into his tunic. Touching him was like touching burning embers, enough to make her flinch each time her fingers brushed against his firm, smooth body.

He cleared his throat. "I might be of more assistance with my trousers." Yes, she needed his help most terribly. This was too much. The man was her husband, yes, but they'd never known each other this way.

By the time Elspeth had returned with word of the wagon's preparation, Alasdair was on his feet and slowly moving across the room with Beitris under his strong arm. "We must make haste," Elspeth whispered as they descended one slow step at a time.

As if Beitris required reminding. Her heart was fit to burst from her chest with its pounding, her head throbbing with the notion of what might occur should Alasdair be discovered. It was enough to steal her breath.

They loaded him into the wagon, with him grunting all the time. "Tis well," he insisted, though his voice shook from the effort.

"Och! There are men in the distance! Coming from the south!" Elspeth hissed. "What are we to do?"

The wagon would travel east, away from the approaching men. "Go," Beitris decided. "Now. Leave me behind. Be quick about it!"

"What if—"

"Do as I say," she demanded of Elspeth. "I shall see to them." Then, an impulse overcame her, and she pressed the back of Alasdair's hand to her lips. "I will come to ye. Now, remain low in the wagon. Go!" She then turned away, walking sedately into the house, as though nothing were amiss.

Though inside, she all but fell apart. Her legs threatened to give way, meaning she had no choice but to lean against the wall for support with a hand pressed over her racing heart.

It was not long before hooves rang out, growing louder all the time. She could only pray they had not taken notice of Elspeth and the wagon—or if they had, they would not give much thought to a single woman driving a team alone. What harm could she bring them?

"Help me," she whispered to no one before opening the door with an inquisitive smile, taking in the sound of four horses trotting through the courtyard. She heard no other hooves, no racing away to the east. None followed Elspeth's progress.

"Good day to ye," she murmured, curtsying. "I am afraid I canna see ye, and I must prevail upon your kindness and patience. What brings ye here?"

The men muttered, whispered, cleared their throats. Finally, one of the men dismounted, landing hard upon the ground. "Mistress, 'tis Sheriff Colin Ramsey, at your service."

She curtsied again. "Aye, Sheriff. My husband has spoken of ye."

"I suspect he has," another of the men snorted in derision.

She turned her face in the direction of that voice. English, though not one of the men she'd overheard in the village. He was quite distinguished, this one. "I dinna believe I've made your acquaintance."

"Quite the lady," the man noted, snorting again. "All you need know of me is my position as magistrate. Edward Longfellow, the name is, and I've been made aware of your husband's involvement with the Scottish army." The disgust with which he spat the last two words told her all she needed to know about him.

"Aye? And what is it brings ye here, then?" she asked, her smile remaining in place.

"We are here to speak to Alasdair," Colin informed her in a quiet voice. She liked this man. He possessed a kind heart.

"Speak to him?" Edward laughed. "Yes, indeed. More than that."

"I am afraid you shall not find my husband on the farm," she shrugged, hands folded before her. Had she washed away every last bit of blood? Would they find her out? "He has ridden out to the highlands. I canna say when he shall return."

"Oh? When did he take his leave of you?" Edward challenged.

"Tis been three days now. He spoke not of why he decided to set out." She lowered her head. "He does not share such matters with me." Let them believe her lonely, left on her own, the blind bride fit for no man.

"Then it was not Alasdair Macintyre who attacked two English agents in the wood this morning?" Edward challenged, his voice sharp as a whip.

"This morning? Which wood?"

She thought Colin snorted softly, but only her hearing would be keen enough to notice.

"The wood near the farm," he explained. "A man with a scarred face shot a bolt through the thigh of one of the men, and knocked the other about the head until senseless."

She clutched her throat. "Such a man in the wood nearby? With my husband so far away?" It was no difficulty to sound frightened, as she'd been frightened since her visit to the village.

"Dinna worry yourself," Colin urged, touching her elbow before taking it in a firm grip. "No harm shall come to ye. We shall send men to the highlands to search."

"How would one hope to find a man on the run in such a vast area as the Scottish highlands?" Edward muttered, his disgust obvious. "We were told the man would be found here, on his farm. That he rarely stepped foot beyond his own borders. He assured me I would find Alasdair Macintyre here."

"He?" she asked, perhaps a bit more keenly than she ought to have.

"It is none of your affair." The magistrate swore openly as he brought his horse about. "If you are lying to spare the man, your blindness will not spare you."

"I ask you to hold your tongue!" Colin barked. "You have no call to speak to the mistress of the house in such a manner—nay, to any woman."

"You might do better to hold your own tongue," Edward

called back. So he was already on his way out from the courtyard. Might she be able to breathe easier? It seemed that way, as the other two men who had not spoken followed suit.

Yet she was not alone. Colin remained beside her, the hand on her elbow tighter than ever. "Ye may do well to clean the blood from the ground near the house," he whispered near her ear. "It seems someone bled a great deal."

She stiffened. "Ah... that is, I..."

"Dinna bother yourself," he whispered. "Ye had best keep him wherever he's hidden for now. Fortunate for us all some men dinna possess keen observation." He left her then, following the others, leaving Beitris all but weeping with relief.

13

———

It was late in the day when the sound of hooves against earth stirred Alasdair from his fitful slumber.

Fitful or not, sleep was the only escape from the pain. For one moment, he resented whoever had come to disturb his respite—until the sound of her voice reached him. "Ye need not fear. I am certain the sheriff led them away from the farm," Beitris whispered. "I feared he would not, but he is a friend."

"How can ye be so certain?" Elspeth demanded in a low voice.

"He saw the blood on the ground, the blood Alasdair shed," Beitris hissed. "I had not thought of it. The magistrate took no notice, thank the Lord. But Colin Ramsey did. He told me we ought to keep Alasdair hidden."

So his blood might have given the entire scheme away. Beitris might have been captured and taken away, all because she'd wished to protect him. If it were not for her idea to hide him in the cave, he might have still been in the house, ready to be captured. Even Elspeth had taken quite a risk, driving the team, racing to conceal him.

He'd given neither of them any reason to take such measures, having been cold and distant for so long. They'd leaped into action without him telling them to do so, to their own detriment if they'd been caught at it.

"I gathered herbs for fresh poultice, and a tincture to ease the pain," Beitris whispered, standing at the mouth to the cave.

"Och, he is in need of it," Elspeth fretted, also whispering. "I asked myself whether I truly ought to leave his side to fetch ye. A man is capable of anything at all when in the grip of such agony."

"I would not call it agony," he grunted, though this was a lie. He'd never known such searing pain, not even when his face had been sliced open.

"Alasdair!" Beitris rushed to him as quickly as she could, feeling her way along the cave's rough wall before nudging him with the toe of her leather shoe. "Ye are awake."

"And ye were clever enough to turn away the magistrate," he murmured, trying to smile. "How ever did ye manage it?"

She shrugged, involved in untying the ends of a length of cloth which she'd gathered together to make a sack. "I told them ye'd gone to the highlands. That angered him, I can tell ye." Was she chuckling?

"Did ye believe ye?"

"Likely not," she admitted. "But t'was enough to send him on his way, which was all I wished."

Never would he have imagined her to possess such strength, such cunning. To have turned away the English magistrate, she must have kept a cool head in the grip of fear. All alone, at that, with not even Elspeth to defend her.

His hand seemed to lift of its own accord, stroking the end of her braid as it hung over one shoulder. Soft, her hair was. Even now, in such anguish, he asked himself what it would mean to run his fingers through it.

"I must return to the house," Elspeth sighed. "There will be questions once the lasses return after supper."

Before Alasdair had chance to speak, Beitris turned to her. "Tell them he's gone to the highlands," she ordered. "We must be certain everyone tells the same story should they be questioned."

What a wonder she was. He allowed himself to relax as best he could, slowly becoming convinced that she had the matter well in hand. He might turn his efforts toward healing, then considering what to do once he'd healed enough to ride. Where might he go after that?

Surely, he could not bring further danger into Beitris's life. He'd done enough of that by now. She deserved none of it. "What shall ye do for yourself?" he asked as she went about unwrapping and sniffing one packet of herbs after another.

"I dinna ken. What about myself?"

"I only mean, how shall ye care for yourself? Ye must take care of yourself as well. Your safety."

"I shall be safe enough," she assured him without hesitation. "Dinna fret. Now. I must apply a fresh poultice to your burns, to keep them from infecting. A tincture for the pain shall follow. Have ye eaten?"

"Nay, t'was the furthest thing from my thoughts," he admitted, feeling a bit chastised.

"Ye shall eat now," she informed him, firm. There was no room for argument, though he was hardly of a mind to argue.

Elspeth rode away in the wagon, promising to return that she might fetch Beitris later. This left the two of them alone, working him out of his tunic as they'd worked him into it. "Ye have already done so much," he observed in a tight voice, settling back against the folded blanket which served as a pillow propped against the cave wall.

"Tis no matter." She ran her hands over his stomach, searching for the bandages which Elspeth had put in place. He inhaled sharply, though not for the reason she imagined. "Have I hurt ye?"

"Nay," he murmured. That was not the problem at all. It was the touch of her hands against his skin.

"Perhaps ye'd best have the tincture now," she decided. "Before I pull the bandages free." Within moments, she'd mixed ground herbs into water drawn from the creek. The lass had even brought a cup from the kitchen at the house. She thought of everything.

"Och, that is better," he admitted after a few minutes. "Quite a strong mixture to work so quickly."

"I did not spare any," she chuckled. "I would wish for ye to be out of pain as much as possible."

"Thank ye." He closed one hand over her wrist as she went about preparing his poultice. "Truly. I can ne'er express what this means. How ye have gone out of your way for my sake."

"Ye are my husband, are ye not?" She spoke with such simple, plain sincerity, it was enough to break his wounded heart. He did not deserve this. He did not deserve her.

He allowed her to go to work, peeling away the old bandage. "Allow me," he offered, cleaning away bits of dried poultice which had stuck to his skin. Once clean, she spread a fresh mixture over his side and was gentle in applying a new bandage. Now that the tincture had run through his blood, he felt much better. As if the very world around him had brightened, lightened.

Next came his shoulder, and the work went more smoothly without pain making each movement agony. "How did ye come to learn this?" he could not help but ask.

"Why are ye surprised? Because I canna see, I ought not have learned to heal?"

"Dinna mistake me," he pleaded. "Ye ought to know by now that I would not underestimate ye. Ye are the most impressive soul I've ever known, man or woman."

She blushed, making her bonnier than ever. Her eyes sparkled when she raised them in his direction. "Ye need not say it."

"I do, indeed, need to say it."

She ducked her head again. "Elspeth taught me, naturally. She taught me a great many things. She ne'er imagined me helpless—just the opposite. She wished to instruct me in all things, that I might be better able to fend for myself."

"A wise woman." Certainly, knowing the lass's father, he would not have taken such pains to see to her educating. "I shall have to offer thanks. Little could ye have known how ye would one day spare my life."

"The time she took was well-spent, then." She smiled.

He realized he'd given her far too few reasons to smile during the course of their marriage. He made a vow then and there to bask in the glow of her smile more often.

If he survived this, and if he managed to avoid capture.

"Ye need worry over nothing," she murmured, applying the bandage to his shoulder. "We shall keep ye safe here. No one shall find ye, and ye shall be well again."

"But the danger—"

She touched his face for the first time since the night they'd met, finding his lips and pressing her fingertips there. "Say no more. Ye are my husband. I will see to it you're safe."

He could not help it. Either the tincture made him take leave of his senses, or it had given him the courage to do what he ought to have done long ago.

Holding her hand in place, he kissed those fingers, then her palm. He placed it against his cheek. "What have I done to deserve a wife such as yourself?" he whispered, the walls between them falling as he reached out with his other hand to gently cup the back of her head.

"Alasdair..." she whispered, though she did not resist when he pulled her closer for a soft, tender kiss. Nor did she stiffen when he closed an arm about her waist to pull her against him.

In fact, it seemed her only concern was for his wounds. "I shall hurt ye," she whispered when he pressed his body to hers.

"Ye could not," he whispered in reply, and neither of them spoke for quite some time after that except to whisper the other's name in the darkening cave.

14

"Mistress!" One of the lasses burst into the kitchen, breathless.

Beitris lifted her head, her hands busy scrubbing potatoes. She'd struggled to find ways to occupy her time and calm her nervousness over the last two days of Alasdair's absence. Keeping the rest of the household away from the cave and unaware of the scheme she and Elspeth endeavored to maintain had been a difficulty.

Now, there was a frantic lass searching for her.

"What is it?" she asked, smiling. She'd smiled enough to make her face ache these past days.

"A visitor," the lass whispered, now standing by her side. She all but shook with fear, the poor thing.

Which, naturally, made Beitris's heart beat doubly fast. "Who might it be?" she inquired, only a slight tremor in her voice now. The magistrate? Perhaps he'd thought better of believing her excuse.

"Bruce Boyd."

She nearly slumped forward in relief. Her father. The least of her worries. "Och, 'tis himself? I have received no word of him these last months. I'd begun to believe he would ne'er show his face here." In fact, she'd reveled in the notion of never breathing the same air as her father. These many weeks away from him had been nearly a joy, even the month in which Alasdair had closed himself in his chambers.

"He is in... a state," the lass whispered. "A terrible state. All but fell from his saddle. The stable lad helped him to the master's study."

"I ought to have known," she grumbled. Her father was in his cups, as ever. How he'd managed to ride all the way to the farm without breaking his unworthy neck was a mystery. She made her way to the study and could all but smell his sour breath before she'd entered the room.

"There she is! My daughter. Married life agrees with ye." He'd already poured himself a fresh drink and drank noisily before continuing. "I ken your husband is nowhere to be found."

What a strange thing to say, so soon. She'd not had the chance to greet him. "Nay," she murmured, more wary than ever. "He is not."

"Where would he be, then? Leaving ye alone. Does he care so little for ye?"

She folded her hands before her. "My husband cares for me a great deal. There were matters to which he needed attend. He has confidence in my ability to manage for myself."

"With Elspeth, no doubt. Surprised I am she isn't trailing behind, as ever." Bruce snickered. "Where would I find her?"

"She went for a walk," Beitris lied again. There was not so much as a twinge of guilt in her heart. "We both enjoy taking the air. The farm is so lovely."

"Ye canna see it."

"I see it verra well. Perhaps better than sighted people could see it," she maintained in a low voice. "If ye have only come to criticize and question and drink my husband's ale, I must ask ye to be on your way. I have matters to manage."

"The lady of the house," Bruce scoffed. "Och, this could be grand again. All of it. A proper keep, a proper clan. So much land. The Macintyre name meant something when my da was a lad, but fools such as Angus Macintyre were content to allow the land to be used for farming, of all things. No guards, no armory. A terrible pity how it has been misused, allowed to fail."

"My husband does not think it a failure. Nor do I. He is content to be a farmer. Tis all he wishes."

This earned a snort, a muttered curse as yet more ale splashed into the cup. "He is a fool, then. All the better for him to be taken as a Jacobite. I did well to speak to that magistrate."

Her mouth fell open, her hands clasping tighter than ever. It could not be. "I dinna... A magistrate?" she asked. Yes, she must pretend not to know what he spoke of. As if she'd never heard the word. "What call would ye have to speak of Alasdair to anyone?"

"Ye misheard me," he snapped.

"I did not." She closed the door, granting them privacy. "Ye might do me the honor of explaining what ye mean. Ye spoke to a magistrate about my husband? Why would ye do such a thing? What business does a magistrate have with him? And what does being a Jacobite have to do with any of it?"

He began to pour yet another drink.

She went to him, flying to his side, in fact, placing a hand over the top of the cup. "Tell me." It was a bark, a command, the sort he would be foolish to ignore.

He knew it well, too, and was quick to set down the pitcher and cup. "What shall I say? Dinna ye ken what there is to be gained here?"

"Gained?" She shook from head to foot, enraged and horrified as understanding began to dawn. No. He could not. He was not as cruel as all that.

"He has all the wealth and land and everything needed to make the Macintyre name mean something once again, yet he squanders it," Bruce snarled, shoving his way past her. She heard him walk to the window, like as not gazing over the lands beyond. "Should anything befall him, all he holds would be passed to myself."

"Yourself?" she gasped, holding onto the table for support as his true meaning became clear. "Ye wish to take his lands, his... all of it?"

"All of it. T'would fall into my hands thanks to yer marriage."

"What... what of myself?" she whispered, struggling to make sense of it.

"What of ye?" he snarled. "Ye would be allowed to remain here for as long as ye wished, but ye could not own anything. Ye are merely a woman."

It could not be. She must be imagining this. How could he be so cruel, so unfeeling? He spoke of his son by law as though his life meant nothing. "Ye revealed him to the English magistrate as a Jacobite in hopes he would be captured and killed. T'was yourself."

"Och, so ye knew it well and pretended ye did not," he laughed. "Clever. Cleverer than I imagined, to be certain."

Shaking with rage, she raised an arm and pointed to the door. "Go. Now. Remove yourself from my presence before... before..."

"I will, at that," he snorted. "I shall make my plans for the estate, in the meanwhile."

There was nothing to be said, nothing which she would not regret in this first white-hot flush of rage. She'd never imagined him capable of such devilry, the cur. Yes, he'd neglected her except in finding a husband, but he'd given her a home and sustenance the duration of her life. She'd imagined him to have at least a shred of humanity left in him.

When she was certain he'd gone, the sound of his horse's hooves fading into silence, she ran for the cave. It was nothing to follow the trail left by the wagon wheels, telling by the sound of the flowing creek and the ever-strengthening scent of spruce how to go. Before long, she smelled a fire along with the spruce, and she knew she'd come near the cave.

"Elspeth?" she whispered after crossing the creek.

A great rustling noise, and Elspeth's whisper reached her soon after. "My dear, what brings ye so soon? I'd not intended to fetch ye—"

She held a finger to her lips, clutching Elspeth's shoulder with the other hand. "Is he awake?"

"Nay, lass, he's slept much of the afternoon. What is it?" Elspeth's hands touched her cheeks, which she'd not realized until then were streaked with tears. She'd wept all along the way to the cave.

The entire sordid tale poured forth in broken whispers. "What shall I do?" she asked on concluding, weak from strain and fear.

"Och, the... beast," Elspeth grunted, thinking better of using stronger language. "I ought to have guessed it. He is capable of all manner of brutish things."

"What shall I do, though?" Beitris demanded. "I canna allow this."

"Nay, ye canna," Elspeth agreed. "Yer first duty now is to yer husband, not yer father. What father he was to ye, that is."

"But I know not how to help it!" Beitris whispered. "If they capture Alasdair, the entirety of his estate will fall into my father's hands. There is nothing I can do about that, either. I am helpless." For the first time in her life, really and truly. Never had she felt so without hope, even when her sight finally failed her.

Then, another thought occurred, one even more dreadful than the others that had raced through her mind as she ran to the cave. "What if Alasdair learns of this? The betrayal. What if he kills my father for it? Ye know he is capable of it. He is fierce and hatred will surely strengthen him further."

"Aye, I ken too well," Elspeth groaned. "Again, ye must decide with whom yer loyalty lies. Bruce Boyd saw to yer care, lass, but now..."

That was not what truly frightened Beitris, though she could not put her thoughts into words she felt her longtime friend would understand. It was not for her father's safety that she feared the most.

It was what might become of her husband should he be discovered as Bruce's murderer.

15

Alasdair asked himself if it was all a dream. If the voices he heard outside the cave mouth were, in fact, those of his wife and her companion.

His fists clenched with rage, and he felt them tighten to the point of discomfort. He could not have dreamed the sensation, nor was he dreaming of the increasing pain in his shoulder and side now that the tincture which Elspeth had provided wore off. It was the pain which had woken him.

In time for him to hear what was being whispered about mere feet from where he lay.

So that was why she'd been married to him! Why Bruce Boyd had schemed to unite his daughter with a Macintyre. He must have plotted it all from the start, scheming to obtain the lands and wealth which Alasdair's father and grandfather had worked hard to accumulate. A man such as himself would never imagine working half as hard, would never wish to put in the time and sweat and devotion.

He was devoted only to himself. And to drink.

And Beitris? To whom was she devoted? He'd been a fool to trust her, to open his heart even the slightest bit. A fine thing, pretending to care for him. Pretending to devote herself to his safety and health. To spend what he'd imagined were the sweetest, most thrilling hours of his life in this cave, pretending all the while to give herself fully to him.

"Fool," he muttered to himself, wishing the men who'd ambushed him had succeeded. Surely, death would have been preferable to this.

No. His jaw tightened, his eyes narrowing in the dark cave, lit only by a dying fire. No, he would not succumb. He would not give Bruce the satisfaction, nor would he allow his deceitful wife to believe she'd convinced him of her faithfulness.

He would kill them both before he'd allow such a thing to come to pass.

"Ye have woken." Elspeth joined him, leaving Beitris standing at the cave mouth. "Yer pain must—"

"Never mind the pain," he growled in a strong voice, causing the woman to jump, startled. "There are worse things than pain. Such as treachery."

Both women gasped. "Ye heard, then?" Beitris asked, dismay heavy in her voice. "Och, husband—"

"Speak not!" he bellowed. It took every last scrap of his strength, but the effect was what he'd desired. Beitris flinched as though she'd been slapped. "Ye need pretend no longer, woman. I ken too well what has been behind your ministrations. Though why ye would wish to spare my life when t'was your father who caused the attack, I canna say."

Her brow furrowed. "Ye know not what ye speak of," she insisted, coming nearer. He wished she wouldn't, for the weakness he'd developed toward her only made him long for her nearness. For the scent of her skin and the feeling of her hair—as soft as he'd imagined—between his fingers.

How that weakness could exist alongside utter loathing was a strange thing, indeed.

"Dinna I ken? I heard the pair of ye whispering, plotting, mere moments ago."

"Ye did not hear all," Elspeth insisted, for once calm and sedate. "Nor did ye see the lass when she arrived, weeping and breathless, having run the entire way with none to guide her. Desperate to see to yer safety, terribly distraught at her father's treachery."

"As if ye would not defend her," he scoffed, waving a hand toward his wicked wife. "Doubtless the two of them plotted this all along. Little wonder he was so eager for the wedding to take place."

"Cease this, immediately." With the determination he'd come to expect from her, Beitris flew to his side and sank to her knees. "I knew nothing of his plotting until this verra day, and he would not even have told me were he not in his cups. He was searching for ye, no doubt. I told him as I told the others, that ye were nowhere to be found. I ordered him from the house, and I hope to never hear his voice again."

"Simple enough to say," he muttered. If only he were stronger. It was no simple thing for a man to rage while weak as a bairn, and nearly as helpless.

"Tis the truth," Elspeth insisted. "I knew nothing of it, either. I ought to have imagined it, but 'tis been long enough since ye were wed that any such thoughts were lost to me. I assumed all was well."

"As did I," Beitris agreed with a firm nod.

Was it true? He wished with all his might that he did not so desperately want it to be true. He wanted to believe Beitris was who she appeared to be, that her devotion to him came from a place of deeper understanding and sympathy. The delicate connection they'd forged, the intimacy they had only just enjoyed—if it were all an act on her part, how could he live with himself?

She found his hand, closing hers over it. There was not so much as a tremor. "Ye must believe me. If ye dinna, I know not how we are to find a way beyond this. All is lost if ye choose to ignore what we are trying to explain."

He looked to Elspeth, brows lifting. "Well?"

"I would sooner cut off my arm than forge a deception with the likes of Bruce Boyd," she snarled, turning her head and spitting on the ground. "Why would I wish for him to enrich himself, at that? He deserves none of it. Besides, I have witnessed his disregard for my Beitris for lo these many years. Why would I allow him to use her this way without speaking up?"

Somehow, that was what satisfied him. Elspeth was not the sort to go along with such a plot. Beitris was the man's daughter, and while she might not love him she might very well feel a sense of loyalty. He'd kept her beneath his roof for years, had fed and clothed her while other men might have been rid of her long since.

But Elspeth owed him no loyalty, and while she'd do probably anything to protect Beitris, she would not have allowed her to be used in such a manner. "Verra well, then," he muttered, chastened but no less furious. "What am I to do about it? The man canna be permitted to live."

Beitris gasped, clutching his arm. "Nay, ye canna!"

"Ye love him still, then," he derided. "I ought to have known."

"Tis not that," she scoffed, bitter. "Tis yourself concerns me. If ye were to kill him, ye would be hunted doubly. How could I spare ye that? How would I protect ye? Do be reasonable."

"He canna be allowed to persist in this treachery!"

"Ye are correct," Elspeth agreed, easing him back against his makeshift pillow. "He canna be. Killing the man would merely make things more difficult for yourself. Dinna fly off in rage. Ye are too weak to so much as lift a sword, at that."

"Dinna remind me," he groaned. It was one matter to be enraged, for pain to dissipate in the face of such anger. Now that his rage had calmed somewhat—thanks to knowing his wife had not plotted against him—the pain made itself known again.

Beitris prepared another tincture. "Drink," she urged, her voice softer now. "Rest. Regain your strength. Then, we might be better able to plan what's to be done."

She turned her head toward Elspeth. "We ought to return before there are questions, as loath as I am to leave."

He caught her arm before she turned away. "Take great care, I beseech ye," he murmured. How could he have doubted her? Certainly, there were still tear stains on her cheeks, revealing the depth of emotion with which she'd struggled before he'd awoken. "Promise me."

Elspeth hurried away, leaving them a moment of quiet. "Aye," Beitris whispered, her palm against his scarred cheek. There was not so much as a flinch from her when she touched him—nor did he flinch away. "I shall take care. And I shall return at the earliest possible moment, at that."

He believed her, and his heart was fuller than he recalled it having ever been as the tincture lulled him into deep, painless sleep. Bruce Boyd would be taken care of, no doubt.

For now, Alasdair had the devotion of a good, true wife to sustain him. It was more than he could ever have hoped for.

16

"It will be no simple matter, keeping the rest of the household quiet about this," Elspeth muttered as she and Beitris knelt in the kitchen garden the morning following the visit from Bruce.

"Ye need not tell me," Beitris whispered. "And ye might do well to remain silent on the matter while so near the house." She felt about for new potatoes and flinched when a worm slid across the back of her hand. Strange, that reaction, but perhaps not so strange when one considered the immense strain she was under.

"Besides," she continued, digging up another potato, then another, "there is no reason for any of them to question his absence. In fact, they are likely glad of it." Though this ought to have comforted her, there was no ignoring a pit in her stomach when she considered how frightened they were of him.

Just as she had once been. There was nothing so frightening about the man, nothing at all. Yes, he had a temper, but it was clear to Beitris that beneath the hard, bitter, ill-mannered image he attempted to impart was a tender, wounded man who possessed a great deal of kindness.

They could not know that, naturally. They did not know him as she did. They could not know how gentle and thoughtful he'd been back at the cave, when they had truly become husband and wife. Just the merest thought of that night made her flush with warmth from head to toe.

"Aye, 'tis true," Elspeth conceded. "They shall believe anything ye tell them, at that. Ye have earned their trust."

Yes, trust which she broke by lying about Alasdair's absence. It was for the best for all of them. The further away they believed him to be, the safer they were.

At least, Beitris told herself as much. She had to. She needed to believe it.

After leaving potatoes and cabbage in the kitchen, they set out to fetch herbs from the wood. The mixture of herbs used for the tinctures had gone woefully low these last days—she did not wish her husband to be in pain when they had means of easing that pain, but this meant running through their supply in a flash.

Beitris sank to her knees in the soft, cool earth, holding handfuls of herbs to her nose that she might identify them better. "Have ye gathered enough heather?" she called out to Elspeth. It aided in sleep when steeped as a tea, and Alasdair needed to sleep as much as possible so he might heal quickly.

"Aye, there ought to be more than enough," Elspeth affirmed. "Willow bark, as well, for the pain."

"Bonny. That ought to do it." She gathered the pouches which she'd carefully lined up before her, tucking them into her apron.

"Ne'er have I known ye to be so determined," Elspeth observed as they started back toward the wagon, left just beyond the tree line. "Ye have been like a woman possessed these last several days."

"Ye spoke the truth. He is my husband, and my allegiance is to him. Is it not proper that I put effort into healing him?" Beitris climbed into the wagon, settling herself on the bench. They would take the herbs to Alasdair, along with food from the kitchen. He would be hungry by then.

Elspeth drew breath as if to respond—but that breath was suddenly cut off, and Beitris understood in an instant that they were not alone. She'd failed to hear the stranger approaching. No, strangers.

Now, there was no doubt. She heard them breathing, heard the team fretting and prancing nervously in place. She'd been too busy thinking about Alasdair to take notice of their surroundings.

A hand grasped her ankle. She kicked out, satisfied at the grunt of pain which resulted, but there was no time to glory in that slight victory when a second man climbed into the wagon and took her about the waist. "Let go of me!" she screamed, kicking and throwing her fists in all directions, her heart hammering wildly, animal instinct giving her strength she would not normally possess.

"Take her!" a man snarled, his voice thick as if his nose had been broken. The man she'd kicked. "She'll soon pay for this."

"Take yer hands from me!" she bellowed, driving an elbow into the gut of the man holding her, scrambling into the wagon once again and taking the reins. She had to get away! The team took off, though she had no way of guiding them. Her only hope was putting ground between herself and the men sent to capture her.

What of Elspeth? What had happened to her? This went through Beitris's panicked, fevered mind as she slapped the reins against the backs of the horses, wind whipping her hair away from her flushed, sweaty face.

Cries from behind her, and the pounding of hooves. They were gaining! She was fleeing in the dark, only the blue sky and the green of millions of spruce needles visible thanks to brilliant sunlight. There was no telling where the team took her, but she urged them to greater speed none-theless.

Until both horses reared, presumably when one of the men on horseback overtook them and blocked the way. The wagon tipped to its side, throwing a screaming Beitris to the ground. Instinct made her roll away from the wagon to avoid being crushed—but this sent her into the path of another horse and rider.

She curled into a ball, hands clasped over her head, frozen as the horse reared and its rider cried out. "Take her!" the man snarled. "The wretch has already been far more trouble than she is worth to me."

Even now, with countless horrors racing through her mind, Beitris recognized that voice. That snideness. The magistrate. "Ye shall pay dearly for this," she spat as two men took hold of her, pulling her to her feet with little consideration for her comfort.

"Yes. I'm certain I shall. Bind her wrists and ankles," Edward ordered. "Do not allow her to get the better of you again. The woman is blind, yet she managed to best you."

"Perhaps ye ought to try for yourself," she growled. "Let us find out whether ye are man enough."

"The cat has claws," he chuckled. "We shall see how brave you are once those claws have been removed."

What was that supposed to mean? Beitris knew better than to ask, submitting to being thrown over the back of a horse and taken away.

Along with her fears for Elspeth were her fears for Alasdair, alone in the cave with no one to tend to his healing. What would become of him? What would he think had become of her?

17

The sun sat overhead, marking midday.

Still, there was no sign of Beitris or Elspeth.

Alasdair's stomach rumbled loudly, reminding him he'd not eaten since a light, early supper the evening prior. As if he needed reminding. The better he felt, the more he healed, the stronger his appetite. This was hardly the time to go without sustenance.

Damn his weak soul. The first thing he'd imagined was her abandoning him. That both women had lied when they'd sworn allegiance. They'd abandoned him, knowing he was at their mercy. That he could not venture far from the cave without risking capture.

It could not be true. He would not allow himself to entertain the notion. "She would not betray me," he murmured to himself enough times that it became something of a prayer. "She would not betray me."

What, then? Had there been another visit paid to the

house? What if the magistrate was not so easily led astray this time? What if he'd never been led astray at all, and had only been lying in wait?

Alasdair stood, bending to avoid scraping his head on the low, stone ceiling. The cave had been his home these last days—he'd lost count of how many, much of his time being spent drifting in and out of sleep. Leaving it was both a blessing and a curse.

For the cave was safety. As much safety as he could be afforded at this time.

Yet Beitris might be in danger, and that meant more to him than his life. What of it if he were captured? So long as he might confirm her safety.

He was still a bit weak, though nothing when compared to the weakness immediately following his injury. Then, he'd barely been able to remain on his feet. Now, he walked out of the cave—slowly, always watching and listening—and crossed the stream with little trouble.

There was an animal in distress somewhere nearby. He heard it. A horse? Neighing, snuffling loudly. He followed the sound, taking care to remain concealed whenever possible. It could be that the animal had been left for him as a trap by one who'd take advantage of his concern.

When he recognized the beast as one of his own—one of the workhorses, in fact, one Elspeth used to haul the wagon to and from the cave—his breath caught. The beast was still hitched to the wagon, but the wagon had over-turned, and the second horse appeared lame at best.

He took off at a run before he could stop himself.

Where was she? Beneath the wagon? "Beitris," he hissed upon reaching the wreckage. "Lass, are ye injured? Speak to me, I beg ye?" Yet when he lowered himself to his hands and knees, peering beneath, he found no one.

It was possible to breathe more freely, but only for a moment. Just because she hadn't been crushed by the falling wagon did not mean she was safe. He stood, looking around for any sign of her. There were pouches strewn about on the ground. Examination revealed them to be filled with herbs and plants. Beitris would not have left them lying about—no, nor the bread, cheese and apples which were gathered in a linen cloth.

She'd been on her way to him. Someone had overtaken her, causing the wagon to overturn and herself to be captured. What of Elspeth? Was she also taken away?

He did not dare return to the house. Someone might be watching, someone who knew he would search for his wife when she did not appear. Where could he go? Who could he turn to?

His head spun, panic and fatigue and hunger combining and leaving him lost. He forced himself to sit beside the wagon and eat what he could, for he'd need every last ounce of strength if he was to find her.

And he knew where to look first.

It appeared the horse he'd believed lame had simply been resting, and he unhitched it that it might graze and perhaps walk to the house. The second horse he unhitched and mounted bareback, turning it east that he might pay a call on his wife's father. The ride would be a lengthy one thanks to the fact that he dare not ride on open road, but he knew his way through the woods and arrived at the stone wall marking Boyd land.

After tying off the horse, he crept as silently as he could toward the stone cottage. It was large, though not nearly as large as the Macintyre keep, and with gathering darkness the men had likely gone inside to take their supper.

It was just as well. Alasdair crouched low beneath a window, listening to voices. There were a number of men eating, drinking, laughing. He continued on, searching for the window that might lead into Bruce's study or bedchamber. Somewhere the two of them might be alone, that they might speak.

Though just how long Alasdair would be able to speak without using his fists remained to be seen. The long ride and the strain of questioning what had become of his wife went a long way toward exhausting him, but the notion of repaying Bruce for what he'd done seemed to grant him miraculous strength in an instant.

He arrived at a silent room, its window open, and managed to climb inside without straining his weak shoulder thanks to the window's nearness to the ground. The room was filthy, unkempt, and he asked himself whether Beitris had once tended the house. It was just as a man such as Bruce would prefer things. Forcing his blind daughter to tend to the cleaning.

It was not long before the man himself stumbled into the room, pitcher in hand and splashing wine onto the straw-strewn floor. Alasdair slipped behind him, wrapping an arm about his neck and tightening it enough to cut off the man's air. The pitcher landed with a clatter at their feet. "Where is she?" he snarled in Bruce's ear, loathing the act of coming this close to him but seeing no other choice.

"Wh—who?" Bruce gasped as he struggled to free himself. It was a useless endeavor, as even while weakened, Alasdair was far larger and stronger.

"Ye know who I speak of. Your daughter. Or had ye forgotten her?" He flung the man away, causing him to hit the wall in front of him, then pinned Bruce against it. "Tell me. Where did they take her?"

Bruce's bloodshot eyes were wide, bulging. "I dinna ken—"

"Lies will get ye nowhere," Alasdair growled, his nose nearly touching Bruce's. "I could kill ye where ye stand for your treachery. She told me it was ye who spoke to the magistrate about me, and why ye did so. Death is too good for the likes of ye. But now, what matters is my wife. Where did they take her?"

"I tell ye, I know not!" Bruce blubbered. "This is the first I've heard of it, I swear on the grave of the lass's mam. I ne'er knew they would take her or involve her. She was not to be touched!"

Could he believe this? "Aye, well, it appears as though ye have been ill-informed. Someone caused her to overturn her wagon—with Elspeth, I would wager. I saw nothing of either woman. There is no other explanation I can imagine."

Was Bruce trembling from fear for himself or his

daughter? Perhaps the latter, more than likely the former. "I knew nothing of it. Had I known—"

Alasdair backed away with a disgusted snarl. "Dinna waste my time with such vows. Ye thought nothing of her, just as ye have ne'er thought of her. Only of yourself. Now, ye see where greed has taken ye. For the remainder of your cursed days, ye shall know t'was yourself who did this."

Bruce hung his head. "What shall be done? What can be done?"

"I canna say. I must find her. But I can tell ye this." Alasdair advanced on him again, fists clenched, murder in his eyes. There must have been, for Bruce shrank back and whimpered at the sight. "I will kill ye with my bare hands if anything befalls her. And if ye speak to anyone of my presence here, I shall make ye wish ye'd never been born. Do ye doubt me?"

"Nay," Bruce breathed. "I dinna doubt ye."

There was nothing more to be said. The man was all but weeping, whimpering like a bairn. He might even have soiled himself—though the effect would have been the same regardless, for he reeked most dreadfully. Alasdair doubted Bruce possessed enough intelligence to pretend so well.

He let himself ought through the window once again and made haste, returning to the horse he'd left behind. What was he to do? He could not go to Colin, being a wanted man as he was. While he trusted his old friend, there was a line between friendship and duty. Colin was a man of honor. There were only so many rules he could be expected to break.

This left Alasdair alone, without a friend to turn to, without anyone he might call upon to look into Beitris's disappearance.

He'd failed her without hardly trying, just as he ought to have known would be the case. He was never worthy of her.

With his heart in his throat, he brought the horse about and head west, toward home. He could not enter the house, at least not until everyone had gone to bed. The fewer people who saw him, the better for all.

18

———

"When are you going to stop lying?"

Beitris did not lift her head. It mattered not whether she did, as she could not see the man. Only the red of his coat, bright and garish if she were able to make it out in a dimly lit room such as the one in which she'd been kept. She could only make out a single candle burning close to where she sat, its flame a single point of light in the darkness.

"I dinna lie to ye," she whispered. How long had it been since they'd throw her into this chair, still bound at the wrists and ankles? She swayed, unable to sit up straight thanks to hunger and fatigue. No, exhaustion.

"I am running out of patience," he spat, shoving her nearly hard enough to send her falling. It would be easy to fall, would it not? To cease fighting, to cease trying. To give in.

Something inside her aching heart would not allow it.

She could not allow this beast to win, to see her break. She steadied herself, biting back a groan. "I dinna know where he is. I know nothing of any men he fought alongside. We were wed after he'd returned to his family home."

She heard him crouch before her, his leather boots squeaking as he did. "Come, now. You were wed months ago. Do you mean to tell me your husband never once made mention of his friends? His fellow Jacobites, those pitiful creatures? Never once did he speak of them?"

"Nay. He speaks little. We rarely exchanged words during the first month of our marriage—hardly ever, in fact. Tis true," she added when the man scoffed.

"I believe you, to a point," he admitted. "From what I hear, he is hardly the type to extend a warm, welcoming hand. So much the better for you that you cannot see him."

She wanted to spit in the man's face. If only she could see his reaction should she find it in herself to do so. But no, that would make things worse. She'd already earned a swollen cheek after being slapped hard enough to make pain explode through her head. It had settled down to a dull throb, but that was dreadful enough.

This was not the time to behave rashly, to give in to her need for vengeance, a desire to make this man's life as miserable as possible. She need remain strong for Alasdair and Elspeth, to maintain a cool head in the midst of so much madness.

"What became of my companion?" she asked, her throat dry and raw, her lips cracking. They'd not given her water. "Elspeth. Where is she?"

"We left her behind," Edward replied, standing over her now. "She might be dead for all I know or care. Would you like me to send a man back for her, to assist her?"

"Of course."

"Then tell me what I wish to know."

She'd expected that. He would not be kind. Even if she gave him this information, he would never bother himself with Elspeth. "I have nothing to tell ye. I swear it. Please, she might be dying. She's done nothing, she knows nothing."

"What difference does it make? You could help her, but you refuse to."

Hot, bitter tears filled her eyes. It was no use. He would never believe her. They would talk in circles until one or both of them fell dead on the spot, and still it would change nothing.

She was no help to her husband, and no help to the woman who'd been a mother to her these many years. She'd failed them both. "Do ye not believe I would tell all if it meant sparing my friend? She has all but raised me. I wish I could help her, truly. I canna. I know nothing. Alasdair never spoke of those times. He wished to forget it, to live simply on the farm. Nothing more."

"A likely story. A Jacobite does not simply abandon their sympathies."

"He cares nothing for rebellion against England, I tell ye!" She was weeping now, but what of it? Let him see how terribly desperate she was, how heartbroken. Perhaps that might convince him. "Even if he does care, he's never spoken of it to me. I canna help ye."

He crouched low again, and now his voice was soft. Almost caring. As a snake's hiss. "Would you not like to eat? You must be hungry. Thirsty, as well—your lips are parched and cracking, your voice is little better than a rasp. Exhaustion will soon set in. You will be unable to sit up. Why torment yourself in this manner? It might all be over so quickly."

"Dinna ye believe I would if I could?" she challenged.

Her head snapped back when he slapped her again, the sound cracking through the room. Blood filled her mouth, pain made the world go darker than it normally was. "You shall tell me what wish I wish to know!" the man bellowed, his face close to hers.

She could not help it. It had to be done.

She spat blood at him, knowing not where it landed but satisfied at his cry of disgust. "I know nothing," she repeated for what might have been the hundredth time. "No amount of striking me will change that."

"I shall kill you for that," he snarled, and it was little better than what she expected. He'd kill her, of course. That was never a question. Once he'd finished tormenting her, he would kill her out of spite. After all, what was she to him? Nothing more than a blind Scottish lass.

With no warning, a door swung open on screaming hinges. "What is this?" a man demanded.

Not just any man. Her father.

She might have known!

"What are you doing here?" Edward snapped. "Be gone with you. This is none of your—"

"That is my daughter! Ye never said—"

"It is none of your concern!" Edward shouted back. "You have no business being here and ought not to have been allowed inside. Be gone with you, and allow me to go about my work."

"This is yer work?" Bruce shouted. She'd heard him shout so many times before, but this was different. He sounded truly enraged. "I had to come and see it for myself. Ye are not a respectable man. Ye have no honor."

"How dare you speak to me of honor?" Edward laughed. "You, who turned over your daughter's husband that you might take his estate? As if I would place any interest in your opinion. Guards!"

Beitris lifted her head, looking in her father's direction. How did he know she was there, or captured at all? Was it Elspeth? Or was it...

Perhaps Alasdair had grown suspicious when she hadn't arrived at the cave. Perhaps he'd gone for help. What if he was captured while trying to find her? She heard her father say her name once, twice, as men dragged him away.

There was no hope. No one would come to rescue her. Alasdair might as well sign his own death warrant if he dared endeavor to free her.

She would die there.

And he would never know she loved him.

19

When a horse approached the cave just before dawn, Alasdair crouched, prepared to fight. It had been many long hours since he'd slipped into his own home and armed himself with the silver dirk which had once belonged to his father, engraved with the name Macintyre. He'd clothed himself as well, and gathered sustenance in the kitchen before any were aware of his presence.

No one knew of this cave, did they? Not that he was aware, at any rate. It could not be Beitris, certainly. Elspeth? He'd neither seen nor heard anything from her since the last visit she'd paid with her charge. The poor woman might be dead, killed without a second thought. After all, she was of no value to the English magistrate or his men.

And she would have fought like a wildcat to protect Beitris. He could not help but smile sadly at the thought.

He was not smiling as he waited to see who the

approaching horse carried. In the thin light of early dawn, nothing but a hulking shape was visible in the mist. A shape which slowly revealed itself to be a person. No. Two people.

Two people he knew on sight.

"She is injured," Colin grunted, sliding from the saddle before helping Elspeth to the ground. Indeed, there was a great deal of blood which had soaked through her linen cap, now dried and stiff. That blood had run down her neck, as well, staining half of her face.

But she was alert enough to instruct Colin on which direction to ride in to find the cave. Alasdair helped her inside, guiding her to lie down just as she'd done for him when he was at his worst. "What became of ye?" he murmured, stroking her forehead.

Her eyes were half-open, but they glittered with a light he'd never seen. Even when she was at her angriest with him, her most disgusted, she'd never looked like this. It occurred to him the injury to her head might have addled her senses. "They surprised us," she whispered, staring up at him. "Surprised... attacked..."

"Aye, so I had imagined," he grunted. Colin fetched a cup of water at the stream, guiding it to her lips when he returned. She drank deeply, sighing in satisfaction once she'd drained the cup.

"Took her? Took my Beitris?" she whispered, clutching Alasdair's hand in her own blood-stained fist.

"Aye. That they did," he admitted. "I dinna wish to frighten ye, but—"

"I knew it without being told. She could not have escaped from so many. Och, I failed her," she whimpered, tears rolling down her cheeks. They did little to cut through the burgundy stains there.

"Ye did nothing of the sort," he assured her. "Rest now."

"We must—" she insisted, trying to sit up.

He guided her into place. "Ye must rest. Do ye recall speaking the same words to me?" he asked with a smile. "I liked them no better than ye do now, but 'tis the truth. Ye can do nothing now but rest and heal."

"I found her at wood's edge," Colin whispered. "Word reached me of Bruce Boyd searching for the magistrate in a fury. He all but confirmed the woman dead, for only death would release her from her duty to Beitris."

"Aye, he was not entirely in the wrong," Alasdair replied, watching the woman. She'd begun to fall asleep. Perhaps that was best for her just then. There was nothing for her to do at the moment, no good she could do them.

"I decided to search for myself and came upon her after an hour, perhaps two." Colin stroked his chin, dark eyes narrowing as he studied Elspeth. "They nearly killed her. The brutes."

"We canna leave her here for always," Alasdair whispered, thinking about the house. "Ye might take her to the house, that she would be cared for there."

Colin's eyes widened. "Have ye been to the house as of late?"

"Aye, during the night."

"And saw ye no sign of any others?"

"I took pains to keep from alerting them. All were asleep."

"Nay, man." Colin fixed a hand on his uninjured shoulder. "All had fled. The house is empty. It was the first place I searched, thinking the old woman might have made her way there. The kitchen hearth was cold, the beds stripped. There was no sign of anyone. They fled, possibly when their mistress did not return. Word has already spread in the village of her disappearance."

They'd gone, fled, frightened. Perhaps it was just as well. Now, they would be safe, away from him. "Let us take her to the house, then, rather than leaving her here. She might be more comfortable in her chambers. Then, we must search for my wife."

Colin appeared pained. "How do ye imagine being able to do so without being captured? Ye are instantly recognizable, and I canna be seen with ye. I am charged with bringing ye in, after all."

Right, and Alasdair would not place him in danger if he could help it. "But she must be freed," he insisted. "Someone must find and free her. Can ye imagine what these men are capable of doing to her? How much harm might already have befallen her? She is helpless, defenseless." His heart threatened to burst free of his chest, it beat so hard. Hard enough to sicken him.

Nothing sickened him worse than the thought of what horrors Beitris might be suffering. All because of him. She was the last person who ought ever to suffer so, yet there she was.

Colin stroked his chin again, staring further into the cave. "There might be a way," he murmured. "Let us take her to the house and make her as comfortable as we can. I dinna much care to leave her alone, but there is much to be done."

20

———

Would that death might come for her and put an end to this torture.

Her feet ached most horribly where the men had stomped on them. There was a persistent, burning ache in her side where she'd been thrown to the floor—had something broken inside her? One of her eyes had swollen shut after she'd been struck too many times.

They'd laughed about that. Laughed because she had no use for her eyes, so what did it matter if one of them had swollen shut?

Every part of her body ached, in fact. Her wrists and ankles, still bound so tightly, had chafed until they bled. Her legs were numb now, but perhaps that was for the best. Her shoulders, burning after she'd been pulled this way and that by men much larger and stronger than herself.

They'd laughed then, as well. Laughed because she

could not see them, could not see where the next blow would come from.

Yet there was nothing she could tell them. When would they finally understand? Why did they insist on continuing with this madness?

What had she ever done to deserve this?

Even now, exhausted and starving and perhaps on the verge of dying, she knew she could not despair. They wanted her to despair. They wanted to laugh at her desperation, her hopelessness. They wished to break her as one would break a stick of kindling. She would rather die than give them the satisfaction seeing her weep or hearing her beg for mercy.

She was alone now. Blessedly alone in this room, empty except for the chair in which she sat. She knew this because she'd not struck any furnishings while falling about the place. How long had she been alone? There was no way of knowing.

One spark of hope remained. If her situation had not changed, if they insisted upon holding her captive, the chances of Alasdair having evaded capture were strong. If they'd captured him somewhere, there would no longer be a need to hold and question her.

If he was safe and far away, this might all be worthwhile.

The screaming of hinges alerted her to the entrance of another of the men. Perhaps they'd rested and were prepared for another hour of torture and laughter. She braced herself, determined to keep her head high.

"Come. We are leaving this place." The man who spoke stopped short. "Och, what have they done to ye? The brutes, the animals!"

"Who...?" she whispered, uncertain of the voice.

She knew the voice that rang out next, however. She'd heard it enough. "Step aside! What right do you believe you have, entering this place with no warning? You might well be sheriff of this filthy pit, but you have no jurisdiction here."

So it was Colin Ramsey. Beitris let out a sigh of relief, slumping a bit beneath the weight of knowing she was no longer alone.

And he believed he'd arrived to free her. What gave him that notion, she wondered.

"I know too well ye have abused this woman, and for no purpose. She was unacquainted with the man when he fought alongside the Jacobites. Dinna ye believe she would tell all after such abuse? Why, she can scarcely open her left eye, and her lips are split open. It must take quite a man to abuse a woman so.

Colin knelt before her. "I shall take ye home, Beitris," he whispered, hands on her chafed, bleeding ankles.

"You shall do no such thing!" Edward bellowed. "Get on your feet, man, and leave this place."

"There is no longer cause to hold the woman here," Colin informed him. The hands about her ankles tightened just enough for her to feel the difference. "Ye shall not find Alasdair Macintyre at his home, nor anywhere else. Not any longer."

Beitris froze, her heart ceasing to beat. "What... how...?"

"What does this mean?" the magistrate demanded. From the sound of it and the removal of Colin's touch, she supposed Edward pulled him to his feet.

"I caught up to him," Colin murmured, distress heavy in his voice. "And when he fought me, I killed him."

How could he say it? How could he simply come out and speak such vile, terrible words? How could he end her life in a single stroke, just as he'd ended her husband's? "Ye canna mean it!" she cried out, sobbing for the first time since her arrival. "He canna be dead! He believed ye—"

"Cease this!" Edward barked before she could continue. "Enough of this weeping. I cannot take the word of a man who also once sympathized with the Jacobites, no matter his position in the community. What proof have you to offer me?"

Yes. Proof. Anyone could say they'd killed a man. He might not have proof. This might all be a ruse. Beitris clung to this hope as she waited, holding her breath.

"I have in my possession his father's dirk," Colin explained. "Stained with Alasdair Macintyre's blood. How else would I have come into the possession of this knife if I hadn't taken it from him? He charged at me, dirk in hand, and I fought it from his grip before plunging it into his heart."

"Stop, stop!" Beitris screamed. Would that she might place her hands over her ears to block out the sound of his voice, but she had no use of her hands.

And she would be able to hear him, anyway. There would be no closing herself off from something so dreadful.

Colin was supposed to be a trusted friend, someone they could both rely on. He'd proven to be the most treacherous of all.

"Ye see, then," he continued in a softer voice than before, "why I have come to free the woman. There is no longer any need to detain her or... beat her, as ye have. She has suffered enough, and now she is a widow. Ye must possess some scrap of decency."

Beitris managed to contain her emotion long enough to listen for a response. "Very well," Edward muttered. "Be gone with you, woman. Never do I wish to see you again."

She did not have it in her to speak. There was no use in speaking, no use in breathing. Alasdair was dead. Her poor, abused, scarred, scorned Alasdair. The kindness, gentlest man she'd ever known or ever hoped to know. How she loved him, still.

And all she had to remember him by were rides and walks and one night in a cave. The only such evening afforded them. It might have been better if she had never known him in that manner, for now she would look back upon what would never happen again.

Colin released her from her ropes and helped her to her feet. When she slumped against him, her legs numb, he lifted her in his capable arms. She had not the strength to demand he put her down, though it gave her no pleasure to be touched by the man who'd ended her husband's life.

"How could ye?" she whispered again and again as

Colin lifted her into the saddle, sitting her sideways before mounting behind her. He offered no reply until they'd ridden for quite some time.

"Hush," he whispered once they were away from any voices or any sound at all saving the singing of birds. "Do nothing, say nothing to reveal what I am about to share. Swear it."

"I swear," she murmured, shaken from her near-stupor.

"Your husband is not dead. He is much alive."

She gasped, then recalled her vow. "I see." It was difficult to keep from bursting into fresh sobs. Could it be? She scarcely dared believe it.

"T'was all a plan we devised together," he whispered. "He gave me the dirk to use as proof."

"His blood, though?"

Colin stiffened a bit, telling her she would not enjoy the explanation. "Tis Elspeth's blood. Dinna ye fret, she is alive," he continued. "Though injured about the head. Injured badly."

"Elspeth," she whimpered, leaning against him now that she trusted him once again.

"The rest of the household has fled," he explained, disgust heavy in his voice. "Though perhaps 'tis for the best, as Alasdair suggested. For the sake of privacy."

"Where is he?"

"He followed the lie ye told. He's ridden into the highlands to conceal himself. He would not tell me where he planned to hide, for t'would only leave me in danger. Tis his way, ye ken. Protecting others at all cost."

Her heart swelled, and the pain throbbing throughout her body mattered not nearly as much. He was alive, and he was safe, even if there was no means for her to reach out to him. He would return to her once the danger had passed.

"How can we thank ye enough?" she asked once they'd reached the farm. "Ye have done all as a friend. A trusted friend."

"Ye need not worry yourself with thanks," he assured her, helping her into the house in spite of her protestations. The feeling had returned to her legs—painful feeling, but feeling nonetheless—and she was more than capable of walking. He carried her up to Elspeth's bedchamber, in fact, the room adjoining her own.

"Tell me of her," she whispered when Colin lowered her to the bed, sitting her up. Elspeth was sleeping, snoring softly.

"She is injured terribly," he admitted. "Alasdair saw to it that the blood was washed from her hair and face. They struck her on the head. She seems herself when she speaks, but there are moments in which she seems not to know where she is or even the year. She believes ye to be a wee lass in some moments, but in others she is well aware of the present."

Poor Elspeth.

Poor both of them, in fact, for they had no one but each other now that the house was empty.

No. Elspeth had Beitris to care for her.

Beitris had no one.

21

———

"Where is the master of the house?" Elspeth asked, sitting up in bed and sipping hot broth which Beitris had just provided. It had taken many weeks of practice for her to learn to fill the bowl and carry it upstairs without splashing her hands, but she had managed.

Just as she'd managed everything else. Six weeks was a great deal of time, after all. More than enough time to learn a great many things, indeed.

Such as the fact that Beitris was not as alone as she'd imagined at first.

With patience, she replied, "Alasdair is not with us. Ye recall, he was called away." Yes, and if anyone visited the house and demanded answer, she might use Elspeth's injury as reason for her confusion. No one would pay heed to a woman who hardly knew the day or even the year from one minute to the next.

Granted, she had made tremendous improvement and could even be trusted to move about the room on her own. Even so, leaving her alone was something Beitris strove to never do.

"Och, of course. How could I forget?" Elspeth was in good spirits today, which was enough to bring a smile to Beitris's face. She'd frowned so many times these long, lonely weeks. Weeks in which there had been no one to manage the cooking and washing, the gardening and gathering. The house more than likely looked quite a fright.

Beitris sat near the bed, hands folded in her lap, her head resting against a pillow. She was tired so often these last several days. It seemed to have come on all at once.

That was the way of it, or so she could recall hearing as a wee lass when the older women whispered of childbearing. The first few months were tiring, indeed, followed by a burst of energy, then greater fatigue in the last stretch.

A child. She was going to bear Alasdair's child. What a wonderous thing.

How she wished she could share this discovery with him, but there was no means of reaching him. After all, she had not the first notion where he'd hidden. Far away, she hoped and prayed. Too far for the English to find him.

At the very least, the magistrate and his men had remained away from the farm. She'd heard nothing of them. Colin had paid a call three times, once a fortnight, and had brought word. Nothing had improved. The magistrate still hoped to gather as many traitors—his word for them—as possible.

Alasdair could not return so long as the man remained in the village. Days passed and the child inside her grew larger with each of them, and its father could not be there to share her hopes and dreams and fears. Yes, fears, for this was her first child and she was alone with a woman she loved very much but who could not be counted upon to provide assistance.

What if she had no one with her when it came time for the bairn to come?

As ever when that question arose—and it arose quite often, sometimes two or three times in the same hour—she had no choice but to push it away with all her might. She could not allow herself to give in to despair or supposition. She could only hope for the best.

"Where has everyone gone?" Elspeth asked. So she was in good spirits, but her memory was poor today. That was normally the way of it. She understood she'd been injured most days and no longer attempted to fight her way out of bed when Beitris thought better of it, but she continually asked questions to which there were no simple answers.

"They ran away. Do ye remember?" Beitris asked, gentle as she could be. "When Alasdair was injured and in danger of being captured. None of them returned, even when word of his... being away spread." Truly, it mattered little whether she spoke the truth or no. There would be no memory of this later.

"Och. Cowardly, the lot of them. Knowing well ye dinna have yer sight," Elspeth muttered. She was correct enough about that, at least.

Beitris smiled. "I canna disagree."

Once she'd finished eating, Beitris gathered the bowl and spoon. "Rest now," she murmured, smoothing back the hair from Elspeth's forehead. It was blessedly cool, something which Beitris was certain she'd never take for granted again after those long, feverish days when she'd feared the woman would die.

"What of yourself?" Elspeth asked, the sound of grunting and rustling of linens speaking of the way she made herself comfortable.

"I dinna think much of myself," Beitris murmured, kissing the tips of her fingers before blowing softly. Elspeth did the same, and Beitris left her alone.

What of her? She was so terribly lonely, so frightened so much of the time. What if someone were to take it into their head to steal? To terrorize the women living beneath the roof of the keep? What if, what if. It never ended.

"Alasdair," she whispered, the sound echoing through the entry hall as she walked to the empty kitchen. Tears threatened to choke her.

Tears which were soon replaced by a gasp of surprise when hooves pounded across the courtyard. She ran to the back door, the one leading to the kitchen garden, a knife in hand. No man would get the better of her, not ever again.

"Beitris? Beitris Macintyre?"

She lowered the knife but did not release it. Her father. She opened the door and stepped out, walking around to the front of the house where her father's horse took water. "What brings ye here?" she called out, relishing Bruce's muttered swearing upon being surprised.

He regained himself in a moment, however, storming to her with his feet pounding on the ground. "What is the meaning of it?" he demanded. She heard the crinkling of parchment.

"The meaning of what, then? Have ye forgotten I canna see what ye are holding?" She scoffed openly, no longer afraid of him, no longer wishing to spare his fragile pride. "I imagine it might be so, as ye have not paid a call in these many weeks."

He scoffed at this, ignoring her complaints. "I hold in my hand a set of papers written and signed by yer damned husband. The cur. The wastrel."

"Alasdair?" she gasped, her heart in her throat. "What do the papers say? Where did they come from? When did they arrive?"

"How the devil would I know, lass? That Colin Ramsey brought them to me, making certain I saw them for myself. Yer husband, it seems, has placed his estate in yer hands."

"Mine?" Her hands were shaking at the moment. She knew it was nothing more than a turn of phrase, but it struck her as amusing. Perhaps she was losing leave of her senses. There was nothing particularly humorous taking place.

"Aye, ye shall inherit all of it upon his death." He thrust the papers her way, all but knocking her to the ground with the force of it. "Only yourself. Never have I heard of anything like it. A woman, inheriting her husband's—"

"Enough!" It came out as a shout, with all the force of her aching heart and her loneliness and her fear, to say nothing of the pride Alasdair's forethought brought her and relief for the sake of the child in her womb. A child who need not be turned away from the farm should anything befall its father.

He had done this for the two of them. Without knowing a child existed, he'd somehow known just the right thing to do. If only he were there then, that she might throw herself into his arms and weep with joy.

"Do ye forget yourself, daughter?" Bruce demanded. "Ye dinna speak this way to me."

"Who are ye to me? My father? One whose selfish, wicked acts led me to this? My husband having run to someplace I canna reach him. My household gone. Elspeth nearly out of her senses. I am alone, thanks to ye." She thrust an arm away from the house. "Go. Dinna ever allow me to hear your voice again, I beg. Or else it shall not go well for ye."

He snorted. "Ye have learned a great deal from yer husband."

"More than I ever learned from ye, I'd wager." She waited until he left, the horse's hooves pounding away until there was nothing but silence around her. She waited until then to weep, to fall to her knees and clutch the papers to her chest and weep for everything she'd lost—and gained.

22

The snows were melting, what there'd been of them. The sun was warmer than it had been all winter long. Spring was on its way.

And still, Alasdair longed for home.

Was this always to be the way of it? Longing for home, unable to be where he wished so dearly to be? More dearly than ever, since home now meant Beitris. He would never have imagined while fighting the English that a year later, he would long to be home with his wife.

If only Colin had upheld his part of the bargain they'd struck. If only he'd given the papers to Bruce Boyd, granting the estate to Beitris. If only he'd continued checking in on her and Elspeth, seeing to their needs, making certain by posting sentries near the farm that none nearby would venture onto Macintyre land to menace the women living alone in the keep.

Nothing like this keep, the one in which he'd taken

shelter these many lonely, cold months. Situated just between the highlands and the lowlands, it had been abandoned for many decades, overgrown and filled with little more than dust, webs and what was left of the animals who'd chosen to shelter there over time.

He was one of those animals, though he had no intention of allowing his bones to lie there until they turned to dust. He would not die. He would not give in. Not when there was so much to live for.

Even if his life was entirely back at the farm, so far away. At least a week's ride, if not longer. He would make the ride three times over if it meant returning to his wife and his home.

The only contact he had with outsiders took place during his brief trips into the village, made only once a week or so. Only to purchase supplies—he'd brought enough coin with him to sustain his needs for at least six months. According to the notches he left in the stone walls of the keep, it had been four months yesterday. Four long months, endless months. The entire winter and then some.

The air was warmer as he walked to the village, his hood pulled up to spare the villagers his scars. Strange, but he so rarely thought of them now. They'd once been the central point around which his life spun, and now he could not have thought less of them. He wished to spare others the shock of seeing them, but nothing more.

How proud his Beitris would be of him when she knew. How proud he would make her, for she deserved to be. She deserved every good thing in the world, including a husband she might be glad to call her own.

How he longed for her. The sunshine of her smile, the warmth of her laughter. Her kindness, her tenderness, her consideration for even the birds and wee creatures of the farm. What a gentle soul she was, and she'd been entrusted to him. How he wished to live up to that responsibility.

If only he had the chance.

"Good mornin' to ye," one of the women of the village murmured with a nod of her head. People tended to keep to themselves here, which was another reason the area suited him. None who'd ever taken notice of him had paid him much mind, and as such if word ever reached them of his being a wanted man, they would not consider becoming involved.

At least, this was what he most fervently hoped. It had been a long time since he'd allowed himself to rely upon the kindness of others, upon their good natures and good intentions. Now, that was all he had to sustain him. Colin's kindness and decency, the strength of the oath he'd made. The willingness of the villagers to pretend he did not exist.

If only Beitris knew this sort of kindness. He'd only prayed once in his life, for one reason: prayers that Beitris would have an easy time of it, without him. That she might find some way to sustain herself. Of all people in the world, sighted or not, he had the most faith in her.

But even the strongest person needed assistance.

There were farms along the river, and the sight of them in the distance caused a tightening in his chest. Men and lads were preparing the fields for planting, as they'd be at home—if the farm was being managed, which he could do nothing but guess at. Guess, and hope, though there was only so much he could ask of his beloved.

He'd be satisfied to find her alive and well and still wanting him, if she ever had. It had seemed that way at times, but after everything he'd put her through, there was no telling how she'd feel for him once he returned. Especially when there was no telling when he would.

If the Lord were good enough and forgiving enough to grant him a second chance at life, he would never want more than to live as a farmer along with his wife. Nothing more than that.

Though it would not be a second chance. It would be a third chance, as he'd narrowly escaped death before. Was it possible to earn a third chance at life? How would he begin to earn it?

"Och, there ye be." The kindly if often sharp-tongued woman who owned the village's only tavern along with her husband reached beneath a table upon Alasdair's entrance. He often stepped in to inquire as to any word from Colin, to whom he'd sent word after settling at the keep. Colin was the only person aware of his whereabouts.

The trust it had taken to send that missive seemed to not have been in vain, for the tavern's mistress withdrew a folded bit of paper sealed with wax. "The seal is unbroken," the woman informed him before he had the opportunity to investigate for himself.

"I thank ye," he murmured before taking the letter to a

nearby table in the dining area, near the hearth that he might see better. Were his hands shaking? Yes, they were, and no man alive would dare blame him for it. This letter might mean the difference between another six months away from home and a reunion with his wife.

It might also mean terrible news.

Breaking the deal and unfolding the paper, he drew a deep breath before taking in the message contained on the page.

Alasdair –

They are gone. All is safe. You might return now. All is well, waiting for you.

Colin

That was all. But that was all that need be shared.

Alasdair bolted up from the table and all but ran for the door in his haste. His heart had wings, as did his feet. He laughed as he ran down the road, clutching the precious piece of paper in his fist. Colin knew better than to elaborate, but there was no need for elaboration.

It was over. The English agents had left the region, leaving the way clear for him to go home.

To the farm.

To Beitris, who according to Colin was well and waiting for him.

To his life.

23

———

"Tell me what ye see," Beitris asked, settling down beside Elspeth on the grass over which they'd spread a blanket. It was a fine, balmy spring day, the sort of day which made remaining indoors seem a silly waste of a gift. Elspeth needed the sun, as well, and fresh air besides.

Beitris had over the last several months given up hope of her beloved companion recovering more than she already had. While her condition was better than in the beginning and, indeed, there were entire stretches of days in which she seemed her old self, it was folly to become comfortable and fall into old habits. For she might just as easily awaken from a brief slumber and declare Beitris a stranger, believing herself fifteen years younger and searching for a wee lass who'd lost her sight.

It was nearly enough to break Beitris's already bruised heart. There was nothing to be done about, however, except to revel in the good days and express as much patience as possible during the bad. After all, how endlessly patient had Elspeth always been with her? It could not have been a simple matter, teaching a blind lass to sew and knit, to cook, to tend the house. The poor woman had spent years trailing behind her charge, making certain each piece of furniture was precisely where it had always been, that Beitris would not fall over it.

If this was the payment required for so many years of faithful service, so be it.

Still, this was a fine day, and Elspeth's voice sounded as it ever had when she described the scene before them. "The lads are turning over earth in the fields," she explained. "And older men. They are all so grateful ye brought them on, my dear. Many men are without labor after the hard winter."

Yes, she could smell the rich earth, could hear their faint laughter and calls back and forth while they worked. Joyful sounds, those, the sounds of men happily engaged in their work.

There was laughter from within the keep, as well, as the small handful of lasses whom Beitris had employed to tend the kitchen and household shared in the joy of a beautiful day. They were airing out the place, shaking the bedding over the windowsills, hanging linens and blankets over the edge that the sun and air might freshen them. The cook and her wee daughter planted in the kitchen garden— Beitris had made a fine disaster of it, as she'd suspected, during those lonesome days when there'd only been the pair of them.

She'd done a great deal of thinking over the winter, Beitris had, spending many hours by the fire with hands crossed over her swelling belly as she pondered the future. The child would need sustenance, to be certain, to say nothing of eyes and hands and caring hearts to look after him or her. Elspeth was a dear thing and would no doubt adore the bairn, but between her addled mind and Beitris's blindness, it did not seem wise to limit the number of household servants in the coming months.

Besides, this was her home. With her husband away and the papers stating Beitris's claim to the estate, she'd taken it upon herself to rebuild what had come so perilously close to falling into ruin. With Colin's assistance, she'd brought new workers in to replace the old and had taken stock of the accounts Alasdair had so carefully overseen.

Her confidence had grown by leaps and bounds, until she'd become quite established as the mistress of the farm. Her farm, hers. For the first time in her life, something belonged to her.

No, the second time. There was a flutter in her belly, a reminder of one who existed therein.

As ever, longing spread through her, a physical ache. How she missed Alasdair. Each new day held the hope that he would come to her. She would awaken and think, *Perhaps this is the day he shall return.*

And every night, before closing her eyes to sleep, she

nursed her disappointment. Yet this did not stop her from feeling fresh hope the following morning. She would never stop hoping, would never stop living for the day he returned. He simply had to.

As this was one of Elspeth's fine days, Beitris turned her head slightly toward her companion. "Do ye believe he shall be proud when he returns? Of all we've done, that is?"

"All ye have done," Elspeth corrected with a smile in her voice. "Aye, I believe he will. If he is not, I shall throttle him, and he shall deserve it."

They laughed together, the sound blending with so much laughter all around them. It was like heaven, or something close to it. As near to heaven as Beitris had ever imagined heaven being. She could bloom here like the many roses waiting to awake from their winter slumber. She could sing as the birds did and there would be no one to silence her, to speak harshly and make her think better of singing again.

There would be no shame, no need to shrink herself down that she might not be in the way.

"The sky is quite blue today," she noted, tilting her face upward.

"Aye, and hardly a cloud. We deserve a warm spring after such a cold winter," Elspeth noted. Beitris wondered whether she truly recalled the winter, or if she merely said this to make pleasant conversation. It mattered little, either way. She sounded happy.

Not for long. "Ye must eat. Ye take far too little food, and the bairn needs nourishment."

"I eat enough for two people!" Beitris laughed. "Truly, my appetite never quiets. I ask myself whether there is one child in my belly or three!"

"Och, three at a time," Elspeth chuckled. "T'would keep us all busy from dawn til dusk."

"And overnight, from what I ken of it."

"Aye, 'tis true. Ye were a darling bairn, truly. Not a bit of trouble, ever. A delight. I pray ye are so fortunate with the child ye carry. Though I fear he or she shall inherit a bit of their father's temper."

Beitris laughed again. It felt good to speak of him, to remember him. It brought him back to her, if only for a bit. It afforded her the opportunity to laugh and smile rather than cry over missing him so dreadfully. "He does possess a temper, does he not? Then again, I have been known to be sharp-tempered, as well. I pray the child does not inherit those qualities."

Then, she thought again. "Though it would not be an entirely woeful thing if a lass were to inherit a temper. A lass needs to speak up for herself in this world, or risk being tread upon. I would not have that for my daughter." She rested a hand on her belly, thinking of the child. Imagining. She'd suspected the child was a girl for some time, though she'd kept these thoughts to herself as she could not explain why she felt this way. Was there something to be said for a mother's instinct?

A mother. A home. A farm. So many things she'd never dared imagine for herself only a year ago. "Do ye recall my railing against the notion of a husband?" she asked Elspeth, linking an arm with hers.

"Aye, I do. I asked if ye didna wish to one day have a bairn of yer own," Elspeth whispered. "Ye were so angry, but I knew. Ye wished verra much for this, though ye dared not admit it."

"I did," Beitris sighed. "I did not believe it possible to have a life, a true life."

She heard the hooved before Elspeth spotted the rider. "Someone approaches," she whispered, obviously upset.

"Dinna fret," Beitris murmured, hoping to soothe her. "Remember, there are many more people coming and going now. We are no longer alone. I am certain 'tis nothing." Though just the same, her pulse beat faster as she worked her way to her feet. It was no small matter now, rising from the ground. Elspeth assisted her.

"Tell me what ye see," she urged, taking Elspeth's arm just as much for her own sake as for her companion's. It was a comfort to the woman, so often confused.

"A man, 'tis clear. He wears a cloak and hood which conceals his face. Tall, large."

A cloak and hood? Beitris gripped Elspeth tighter than ever. "Is it... could it be...?" she breathed, tears in her eyes.

"He lowers the hood," Elspeth whispered—then, she shouted, "Tis himself! Och, my dear! Tis yer husband!"

In that same moment, Alasdair called out. "Beitris!" His voice carried across the fields in which heather would soon grow. The horse's trot became a gallop, hooves pounding just as Beitris's heart did the same.

Within moments, she heard the horse come to a stop nearby, heard Alasdair dismount and rush to her. She threw her arms around him and wept openly, gustily, happier than she'd ever been at any moment of her life.

"My love," she sobbed, clutching him, afraid he would leave her again if she did not hold on tight. "My love."

24

———

Alasdair held his wife, tears soaking into her hair. "My love," she sobbed against his chest. Her love. Another tear rolled down his cheek. So she'd loved him as he loved her. The question he'd asked himself countless times as he'd ridden down from his hiding place was answered at last.

"Och, my darling," he murmured, kissing her forehead, her cheeks, holding her beloved face in his hands and drinking in the sight of her. "Ye look well. Ye look…"

Then, his senses returned at last. He had not taken notice at first, too overjoyed to find her waiting for him, too desperate to hold her again. He stepped back, hands on her shoulder. "My God," he whispered, unable to believe it at first. "Beitris, ye…"

"I carry your child." She took his hand, gentle, tentative, and placed it atop her swollen belly. "Our child."

As if his homecoming were not already emotionally overwhelming. "A child? A son or daughter?"

She laughed softly. "'Tis the normal way of it, aye."

He pulled her in for another embrace, though more gently this time. She was a precious thing, ever more precious thanks to the life she carried inside her. "My dear, my darling," he whispered in her ear. "And all alone."

"Not so alone," she corrected with another laugh. "Do I appear alone to ye?"

He looked to Elspeth, who wept into her apron. "'Tis a bonny thing," she beamed. "Having ye home. She has missed ye so terribly. We worried so."

He patted her shoulder, smiling with affection. She seemed well. "'Tis far better ye appear now than ye did when I last saw ye."

Yet Beitris stiffened beneath the arm he'd wrapped around her waist. "She remembers little," she whispered for his benefit alone, and his heart sank. So she had not recovered entirely.

"Elspeth, ye might inform the cook we have another body to feed," Beitris urged, still in tears. "The master of the house has returned."

"Aye, I shall at that." Elspeth made haste, perhaps as much to complete her task as to give the two of them a bit of privacy.

Beitris turned to him, hands roaming over his face. How strange, remembering a time when he would have flinched away from this. Now, he would have stood in the same place for hours, allowing her to see him as clearly as she wished.

"Ye are thin," she observed with a frown. "Ye have not eaten as ye ought to. We shall be certain to feed ye abundantly."

He kissed her hands. Was this a dream? Could it be real? "There are workers in the fields," he observed now. "And work being done in the keep. Have ye managed this all on your own?"

"Aye." She all but glowed with pride. "I have at that. Colin has been a tremendous help, mind ye. Ne'er could I have made sense of the accounts were it not for his assistance. Elspeth... I canna trust her with such matters, it pains me to say." Some of the light left her eyes.

"Tell me of her," he urged, leading Beitris to a wooden bench outside the keep.

She shook her head, clicking her tongue. "There are good days, and there are poor days. Today she remembers herself, and she remembers me. She remembered ye, as well, which gladdens me. There are times when she awakens with no memory of the last year, or the last fifteen. I ne'er know who I shall meet from one day to the next."

He groaned, silently cursing the men who'd injured her. "The poor woman. It pains me to hear of it. She did no harm to any."

"She canna live alone now, not ever," Beitris whispered.

"Naturally." He looked at her, surprised. "Why do ye feel the need to say it?"

"I—I canna say. Tis a great responsibility, is all. I would not expect ye to—"

"Nonsense!" He held her hands in his, sitting near enough that they touched at the knee, the arm. "My Beitris,

Elspeth shall always have a home here. She may not carry Macintyre blood, but she is of my family, nonetheless. Just as much as ye are my own. She need ne'er be alone, not for the rest of her days. She has earned her rest now and deserves to have others care for her the way she always cared for ye. Ye might cease fretting for her."

A fresh tear sparkled on her cheek. "Truly? The pair of ye rarely got along."

"That was the past, and I was a different man," he reminded her. "Besides, I feel the two of us reached an understanding long ago. Before I left ye."

Sorrow touched his heart then, and he could not help but gaze at his wife's rounded belly. His child grew inside her. "I ought ne'er to have run away," he muttered, angry with himself now. "I left ye with all of this. A wounded woman, a child on the way. All alone. I failed ye when ye needed me most."

"Tis untrue!"

"Tis true enough," he insisted. "Tis my duty to protect ye. To provide. I left when ye needed me most."

"Ye left because there was no choice. They would have killed ye. I know it. I would rather ye hide for half the year than remain here under some pretense of protecting me. T'would have been I who protected ye, dinna forget."

"But... all alone..."

"We survived," she reminded him. "And now, the farm is thriving again, and spring has come, and all is well. Let us not waste this precious time together in mourning the time we lost. T'would mean the loss of more time, which would be a greater pity."

There was a firmness in her voice which told him to keep further reproach to himself. The lass had a point. To argue back and forth over whether he'd been wrong or right wasted the time they now had together. How precious that time was.

How precious she was. He stroked her hair, as soft as he'd remembered it. "Ye said ye loved me," he whispered, afraid to believe it but unable to resist. "Was it true?"

Her cheeks colored. "Aye, 'tis true," she murmured, ducking her head. "I could not help myself. I do love ye, most terribly. I knew it before ye were injured, but I could not find it in me to speak the words. I suppose I was afraid ye would laugh or scoff."

"Ne'er would I scoff at ye," he smiled. How dear she was. "Not for any reason."

"Ye have scoffed before," she reminded him, perhaps a bit sour though with humor in her voice. "Many times, in fact."

"As I told ye, I was a different man then. I've changed so much. Have ye not noticed? And 'tis thanks to ye."

"How so?"

He drew her close, and when she rested her head upon his shoulder he was certain no man had ever known such peace and contentment. Truly, this was what he'd waited for all those lonely days and long, cold nights. "Ye gave me someone to love. To devote my life to. A reason to believe there was something in life worth living for—ye must have known long ago that I gave up all hope before we met."

"Aye," she whispered. "I'd suspected as much."

"I was certain I could only be a disappointment to ye as a husband. Elspeth took me to task, as well."

"How did she do that?"

"She accused me of imagining ye to be useless as a wife. Told me I did not consider ye enough. And she was right. I did not. I imagined ye as just another trial to be borne. Never again will I make such a mistake." He sighed, thinking of the woman who would now be in his care for the rest of her life. He owed her such a great deal. She'd raised Beitris, helped her become the woman who now sat at his side. She'd helped save his life, as well.

He looked around, smiling with pride at all she'd accomplished without his help. "What a wonder ye are. How could I ever have imagined ye as anything else?"

"I did what needed doing," she shrugged. As she would, ever modest.

She sat up then, looking to him with teeth biting into her lip. "What if they come back?" There was a tremor in her voice to match the quivering of her chin.

"Did they harm ye?" He'd forgotten to ask, too overwhelmed by the surprises awaiting his arrival. "What did they do?"

"Tis unimportant now."

"Tis important to me."

She shook her head. "Nothing I could not heal from. A few bruises, a split lip. Colin can tell ye of it, if ye wish to hear, as he rescued me from them and brought me home. At least the bairn was unharmed—I was unaware of her existence then, of course."

In spite of the ugly images running through his imagination, he could not help but smile. "Her? Are ye so certain, then?"

The tiny giggle that slipped loose was nearly enough to make him burst with joy. "Aye, I have a suspicion. I canna explain it."

"Nor do ye have to." He kissed her softly, gently, with all the love he'd held back for far too long. Perhaps it was time to forgive, or at least to put the past behind him. Reflecting on what the magistrate's men had done to his wife while demanding to know where he was hidden would only shrivel his soul until he was no better than the man he'd been prior to his wedding.

Hard. Cold. Bitter and resentful. Angry at the entire world, at God himself. Compared to the lightness of spirit he now enjoyed, the sense of peace and fulfillment when he considered being a father, a family man, he might as well have been an entirely different person.

"I shall ne'er leave ye again, I swear it," he whispered, her forehead against his cheek. He closed his eyes, reveling in the sweetness of being near her again. "If the English are to return, we shall manage it then. But I will not sacrifice my happiness to fear of what might or might not occur. Besides, we can manage anything together. I would face anything so long as I had ye by my side, my dear, sweet Beitris."

It occurred to him that he had not come straight out with it yet, and so he cupped her face in his hands and whispered, "I love ye, Beitris Macintyre. Ye are all of life to me. There is nothing without ye. I shall never be able to fully repay everything ye have done. Bringing me back to life, giving me something to live for. I could ne'er love ye enough, not if I had a hundred years."

He touched his forehead to hers. "But I swear on my life, I shall try. Every day, I shall try."

"I need nothing more than that," she beamed before he kissed her again.

EPILOGUE

"How many potatoes have ye dug?" Elspeth asked, two rows down in the kitchen garden.

Beitris ran her hands over the pile by her side. "Twenty, though they are small. Perhaps I ought to dig more?" She intended to but knew well that asking her old friend for advice made her feel important. While she was never truly aware of why she'd become forgetful and confused, there were days in which she knew there was something different about her now. Bolstering her confidence was one of Beitris's chief concerns at times like these.

"With the way ye have been eating, lass, ye might want to dig another twenty," Elspeth chuckled. "I shudder to imagine how large the bairn is now. Ye might have a difficult time of it in a fortnight or so."

"Dinna frighten me!" Beitris laughed. "Besides, I am strong, and healthy. I have no reason to fret."

"Ye know I merely jest," Elspeth reminded her. "Aye, a few more should suffice."

An earthworm slid over the back of Beitris's hand as she dug, and she smiled to herself. "Forgive me for disturbing your home," she whispered, patting the ground to find the next mound beneath which a young potato grew. This was their first small harvest, little more than two months after the cook and her charming daughter had planted slices of old potatoes in neat rows which stretched out behind the keep.

The bairn kicked, as was so often the case now that her time was drawing near. It seemed there was never any end to the activity in her womb, and she often spent great portions of the night lying awake as the bairn flipped and kicked.

Yet she welcomed it. Her child was alive and thriving and anxious to be out in the world. For her part, Beitris was anxious to meet the bairn. To perhaps scold them for costing her so much sleep, as well.

Elspeth helped her to her feet—no small task now that she was so very large—and gathered the potatoes. "Sit and rest in the sunshine," she advised. "I shall take these inside. Alasdair approaches from the fields."

Yes, Beitris could hear him now. She turned in his direction with a smile. "How goes it?" she asked. "Are the young plantings growing well?"

"Aye, they are at that. The men did a fine job of it."

In spite of this positive announcement, she frowned. His voice was heavy with something more than fatigue.

"What bothers ye? Dinna waste time pretending nothing does."

"I would ne'er dare," he said. "I know better. Take a seat, here." He guided her to a long bench along one edge of the garden, though she needed no assistance. The entire garden was a map in her head, each row marked, her footsteps having worn a path down the length and breadth of the patch of land.

She lowered herself slowly—that, she appreciated assistance with managing. "Your back aches," he sighed, pressing a hand there. "Shall I rub for ye?"

"Perhaps later," she smiled, patting his hand. "What is it ye wish to tell me?"

"Frankly, I dinna wish to speak of it, but ye do need to know."

Darkness settled over her. "What? The English? Have they—"

"Nay, nay," he insisted. "I ought to have assured ye before now. They have not returned. We have nothing to fear."

She heaved a sigh of relief. "What, then?"

"A rider approached earlier, carrying a letter from a solicitor in Edinburgh."

"Edinburgh? Do ye have family in Edinburgh?"

"Nay, my love. T'was yourself who did. Your father. He... passed away."

The news made her gasp. Truly, she had scarcely given him a moment's thought since that day in the courtyard, when he'd thrust the papers at her. When she'd ordered him away and told him she hoped never to hear his voice again.

Now, she never would.

"I am sorry, my love," Alasdair murmured, stroking her aching back which did not seem to ache so much anymore. "I remember how conflicted my feelings were after my father's death. I was still deeply angry with him for forcing me into marriage, but I could not help mourning."

She nodded, the lump in her throat making speaking impossible. Yes, that was precisely the combination of conflicting emotions. Anger and resentment. The memory of all he'd done for her, if grudgingly. He might have abandoned her, sent her away. Abused her.

"The rider brought a letter from Bruce, addressed to ye. Would ye like me to read it to ye?"

Now, the lump in her throat threatened to choke her. She nodded, sniffling. "If ye would," she whispered. "Please."

He unfolded the paper, clearing his throat. "My daughter," he began, speaking slowly. "I thought it best not to tell ye of my riding to Edinburgh. I admit, I left in a fury when last we met. I was too glad to ne'er set eyes upon ye again. Now, after months spent thinking and after growing ill, I understand the folly of my actions."

Beitris drew a broken breath, tears threatening to break free. "Go on," she insisted when Alasdair touched her knee. "Please."

He sighed before continuing. "I was a terrible fool, my daughter. I treated ye unjustly. I might blame my actions upon many things—losing your mother, fondness for drink —but truly, the blame rests upon my shoulders. I know I have little time left to me, and what weighs most heavily upon my conscience is what I did to ye, and to Alasdair. I ask your forgiveness and hope ye might find it in your heart to pray for my soul when ye receive word of my death. I shall pray for ye, and your husband, and the life you spend together. I hope ye know many years of happiness, and many children to bless your union."

Beitris wiped away her tears, nodding slowly. "He saw the truth of it before the end, which I suppose is the best I could hope for. I pray his soul finds peace."

Alasdair placed an arm around her, and she was grateful to lean into his embrace. With her head on his shoulder, she remembered so many things. How she'd hated the man, how she'd resented him for so long. If only he could have seen the error of his ways before then. If only they could have made amends before it was too late.

"Ye are a better person than I could ever hope to be, my dear," Alasdair murmured before kissing the top of her head. "And ye might verra well always be."

"Ye are a good man. Dinna tell yourself otherwise," she chided gently. Then, a flutter inside. "Quick!" she whispered, taking his hand and placing it on her belly. She touched his face, feeling his broad smile when the bairn kicked against his hand. The smile of a proud father.

Life went on, t'was the way of it. One life ended, another was about to begin. This child would receive more love than any child in history, she knew. Between its parents, Elspeth and the household, there would never be an absence of love and affection.

Just as it should be.

"Tell me what ye see," she suggested. This was how they'd forged their first tentative connection, when he'd described their surroundings that she might see the world as he saw it.

He settled back against the fence behind them, still holding her in one arm while he patted her belly with the other. "The sun has begun its descent," he murmured. "The light is golden. There is a haze of green across the fields, as far as the eye can see. New life. The lads are coming in now, and the men who supervise their work. They shall take their supper and sleep well after a day's labor. All is peaceful and calm."

"Perhaps we should take a walk to your tree," she suggested with a smile. "It has been far too long since we ventured there."

He chuckled softly. "Aye, we ought to. The creek will be warmer now. Ye might soak your feet in it. I know they ache terribly when they swell."

He always considered her. "Perhaps in the morning," she replied. "I am tired now. It has been a good day."

"That it has." Another kiss on her head. "There have been so many good days."

"And there are more to come," she predicted as another strong kick made them both laugh. "Good, busy days," she amended.

"Aye. I have no doubt my daughter shall keep us both on the run."

"So ye are so convinced the bairn is a girl?" She touched his face, feeling him smile again.

"I know better than to doubt ye, my wife." He kissed her palm, holding it to his cheek. The scarred cheek, the one which had caused him so much pain and bitterness. Beneath those scars was the man she loved, a man whose beauty ran far deeper than anything on the surface, visible to the rest of the world.

Though her eyes were of little use, she saw what existed beneath those scars. In her husband's good, true heart.

How wondrous life could be.

KEEP READING for an excerpt from the next book in the series!

A HIGHLAND INHERITANCE

Book Two of the *Highlands Ever After* Series!

An English heiress has no cause to live in the Highlands. Or does she...

Sheriff Colin Ramsey simply wants to keep the peace in the territory. He doesn't want to have to enforce the Tartan and Dress Act of 1746. Nor does he want to babysit the feisty Highlanders that seek to create chaos and defy the laws—regardless how unjust said laws might be.

He doesn't like complications.

Enter Iona Douglas, who brings complications in spades. This stubborn Englishwoman has inherited Scottish Highland property. She scandalously refuses to follow rules or suggestions. She insists—quite stubbornly—on brushing off advice in this lawless land.

If only there weren't feelings involved.

If only she wasn't irresistible.

Colin's problem is figuring out how to keep the lass alive when she seems hell bent on ending up dead.

CHAPTER 1

It was with a heavy sigh that Colin Ramsey slid from his saddle in front of the home belonging to Alasdair Macintyre and his wife, Beitris. He'd looked forward to this visit all through the day, as one would look forward to a reward at the end of a trial.

As of late, every new day had presented a trial.

The early May air was warm, and the fact that the sun sank later with each passing day spoke of the summer to come. If anything, the past winter would be a blessing of sorts. The likelihood of the people whose safety was his responsibility staying indoors and out of trouble was higher when the snow flew.

Now? There was no keeping the troublemakers of the village behind closed doors, which left the life of a sheriff in disarray.

This had been the way of it, ever since word of the banning of tartan had been passed down and spread throughout the land. According to the Act of Proscription, it was illegal as of the previous August for any man to wear the colors of their highland clan, and the punishments for doing so were severe to a degree which turned his stomach. The English were not satisfied at having beaten back the Jacobites. They wished to send a message while suppressing further uprisings.

Unfortunately, this act had only served to further inflame tempers which had already been near the point of boiling over. Residents of the village and surrounding lands had gone from disbelief, to disgust, to outright fury. There were fires set, messages written in mud or even blood along stone walls, none of which were precisely favorable toward the English. Not that Colin expected anything less—he was hardly in favor of their rule, either.

Yet he could not allow his personal opinions to interfere with the job he'd been selected to perform. He was a man who took his duty seriously, who would not allow his territory to be overrun either by the English or by resentful Jacobites and their sympathizers.

This hardly made him a popular figure, though he expected nothing less.

Every muscle of his body ached from being held in tension for months on end. It seemed he'd done nothing but frown or scowl for as long as he could remember. Having to scold longtime friends—or do worse than scold —had worn his nerves thin to the point of nearly breaking.

Which was why he had so looked forward to supper with the Macintyres. Not only were they of the same mind as he, but Alasdair had fought alongside him against the English. They were sympathetic to the same cause.

And Alasdair was a reasonable man, unlike some with whom Colin had dealt since the proclamation came down. Certainly, Colin expected the men to be furious, outraged at being denied the right to display clan pride. Yet he would not do foolish things such as wearing his tartan in public, riding through the center of the village and singing at the top of his lungs to draw attention. That was just one of the challenges Colin dealt with during that day alone.

Beitris laughed gently when Colin recounted this tale. "Forgive me," she chortled behind her hand. "I know I ought not laugh. It must be a terrible hardship for you."

Colin couldn't help but to smile at her, though she could not see it. For a woman without use of sight, she possessed a tremendous deal of grit, strength. He admired her more then he could say. She'd seen to the farm coming back to life while attending to a sick, old woman, with no one to help. Colin had checked on them from time to time, but much of the work had been done by Beitris.

All this, without the use of her sight. Without her husband, who'd been forced to flee the English. And while carrying a child which now caused her to walk with a slow, plodding step, swaying back and forth while holding a hand to her lower back. She had all the strength of the most formidable warrior.

He would forgive her nearly anything, he imagined.

"I suspect I would laugh myself, were it not that I needed to bring the man in," Colin admitted with a rueful chuckle. "Truly, he made quite a sight of himself, dressed from head to toe in his clan tartan. And only that. Head to toe."

"Were there any witnesses?" Alasdair asked, passing a platter of sizzling meat across the table.

"Certainly, and they cheered themselves hoarse," he assured them. "Part of me wished I could cheer along with them."

The scar running down one side of Alasdair's face twisted even further when he scowled. "It must be trouble for you, going against what ye know to be right in service of your position."

Colin shifted in his chair, uncomfortable with the direction which their conversation had taken. "Tis not a simple matter," he conceded, sopping up rich, flavorful juice with a hunk of bread. "But I have a duty, and I must abide by it. Remember, my position is perhaps the only reason I was not as avidly pursued as yourself when the magistrate came through."

Beitris stiffened, and instantly Colin regretted ever mentioning it. She had never explained what had been done to her during the harrowing hours in which she'd been held captive while being questioned as to Alasdair's whereabouts, though she hardly needed to. He'd seen the results with his own eyes, and it had been enough to sicken him.

Alasdair nodded slowly, his brow furrowed. "What are ye doing with the men who wear their tartan so brazenly?"

A sore question. Again, Colin shifted in his seat. Should

he tell them? It might put them in an uncomfortable spot if he did—the less they knew, the better for all involved.

But these were friends, and he could not help but wish for them to think well of him. He was merely a man, a man with no family and a few friends worthy of the title. He did not wish for this couple to believe him traitorous or coldhearted. "Until now, the worst I've done is issue warnings. I dinna expect them to be heeded, but I can at least say I made it known such behavior would not be tolerated."

Beitris passed behind him, laying a gentle hand on his shoulder as she did. A silent message. He knew she would understand, if no one else. That she would feel sorry for him, though it normally disturbed him to no end to be pitied.

Then again, he had never faced a challenge such as this one. Torn between love of his history, his people, and the duty he had to a crown he cared nothing for except to hate its influence in his beloved homeland.

"I fear this shall soon devolve further," he confessed. "Men are gathering in secret, quietly, plotting against this latest outrage. I canna allow it to happen."

Alasdair thumped the table with one fist, scowling. "If there's anything I might do to assist ye, dinna hesitate to speak of it."

"I would not expose ye to danger," Colin vowed, perhaps more for Beitris's sake than for Alasdair's. "Ye are a family man now, with so many who depend upon ye. I would not wish to make life difficult for any of them."

"You are a good man, Colin Ramsey," Beitris murmured. "Truly."

"Dinna overpraise him," Alasdair chuckled before rising to help his wife into a chair. "Ye must rely on the lasses in the kitchen and not take so much upon yourself, my dear. Ye must rest."

She scoffed at this, though Colin noted the expression of relief she wore once she'd taken a seat. Alasdair was quick to place a cushion behind her back, hovering over his wife as though she were something rare and precious.

To Alasdair, Colin supposed, she was. Quite precious, indeed. Not for the first time did Colin ask himself what it would mean to find a sympathetic person awaiting him upon returning from a punishing, difficult day. What would it mean to have her ask after him, to fret over his working so hard? What would it mean to hover over her as his friend did over his wife, to guard her with his life and to look forward to the birth of his child?

Silly thoughts. The sort he rarely allowed himself to indulge in, the sort which rarely ever occurred to him. Only when in the presence of a pair who truly loved each other did he give a thought to marriage or domestic life. Perhaps it would be best to avoid this particular home for a time— especially once the bairn came to be, which would only make him long for something that was not his.

Never would he speak these thoughts aloud. Not for anything. He was a man to be respected and feared, not one who gave himself over to flights of fancy or longing for a life that could never be.

Once Beitris's comfort was seen to and one of the lasses from the home's modest kitchen came to tend to what was left on the table, Alasdair led Colin to his study that they might speak privately on the matters in the village. While he respected Beitris and gave credit to her intelligence, he did not wish to worry her with the truth of the troubles he'd seen.

Alasdair poured a healthy amount of ale into a cup and thrust it toward Colin. "Drink, man. Tis clear ye are in need of one."

Colin accepted it, and gladly. "Tis more difficult by the day to contain them." He knew he need not explain what he meant, nor whom. "I fear the village will become a verra dangerous place if they who live within canna control their outrage. I canna lock everyone away, yet 'tis what they shall wish done." No need to say who he meant in this case, either. It was clear enough without the words being spoken.

"Aye, I suppose so."

"We canna have their return," he muttered, staring out through the window behind Alasdair's desk. "I will not have it. I must keep them away. Tis not been nearly long enough they've been gone from this area. And with ye—"

"Dinna concern yourself with me."

"I do concern myself with ye, if 'tis all the same," Colin barked, perhaps sharper than he ought to. What else was there to do when the man seemed determined to argue? "Either I concern myself with ye now or I do it when ye are forced to escape again. If 'tis all the same to ye, I would rather not."

"Forgive me. I did not—"

Colin hung his head, then shook it slowly back and forth. "Nay, nay. Dinna apologize. I am tired, and fearful. It pains me to say it, but 'tis the truth."

"Perhaps this will blow over as a sudden storm," Alasdair mused, staring into his cup with a wry expression. "The sort which seem to be the end of the world when at their height, but ne'er cause damage than canna be undone."

Colin snickered at this. "An old spruce once toppled over in one such storm and punched a hole in our roof when I was a lad."

"But it could be undone," Alasdair reminded him. "Perhaps this is the time for more than just warnings."

"Aye," Colin groaned. "It could verra well be."

And with each of the kinsmen he locked away, his guilt would grow. The sense of betraying his people, his blood. He was a traitor to them, yet the alternative of an area crawling with Englishmen eager to make an example of the rebellious highlanders was far worse.

Short of praying for a miracle, there was nothing to be done but his duty.

I hope you enjoyed *A Highlander's Redemption*!
Next in the series... *A Highlander's Inheritance.*

For more Aileen Adams works, click here!

Sign up for the newsletter to be notified of new releases.

Click on link for
Newsletter
or put this in your browser window:
mailerlite.com/webforms/landing/o3j5xo